Not Just Proms & Parties

Rica's Summer

Not Just Proms & Parties: Rica's Summer

Published by Lobster Press™
1620 Sherbrooke Street West, Suites C & D
Montréal, Québec H3H 1C9
Tel. (514) 904-1100 • Fax (514) 904-1101 • www.lobsterpress.com

Publisher: Alison Fripp
Editors: Alison Fripp & Meghan Nolan
Editorial Assistant: Molly Armstrong
Cover Design: Audrey Davis & Jenn McIntyre
Graphic Design & Production: Tammy Desnoyers

We acknowledge the financial support of the Government of Canada through the Book Publishing Industry Development Program (BPIDP) for our publishing activities.

We acknowledge the support of the Canada Council for the Arts for our publishing program.

Library and Archives Canada Cataloguing in Publication

Penny, Patricia G., 1953-
Rica's summer / Patricia G. Penny.

(Not just proms & parties)
ISBN-13: 978-1-897073-45-2
ISBN-10: 1-897073-45-3

I. Title. II. Series: Penny, Patricia G., 1953- Not just proms & parties.

PS8631.E573R52 2006 C813'.6 C2006-900723-3

Printed and bound in Canada.

With thanks to my sisters, Marion and Sheila, for sharing childhood and teen years with me, and for being such great friends now; to my children, Craig and Laura, who are an endless source of pride and inspiration; and to my husband, Bob, without whose constant support and encouragement I would still be saying, "I should write a book one day." I love you.

– Patricia G. Penny

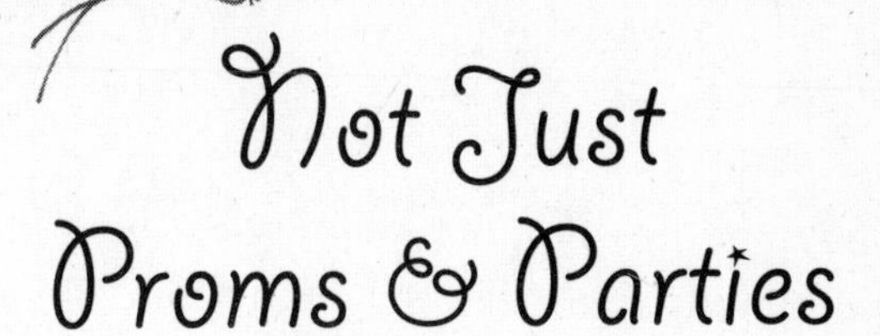

Not Just Proms & Parties

Rica's Summer

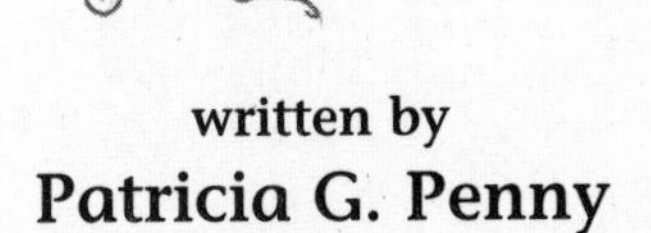

written by
Patricia G. Penny

Lobster Press™

Chapter 1

Italy. The Riviera. Maybe the Caribbean. Just once Rica wished that they could go on a *real* vacation.

She sat in the back of the van and turned up the sound of her iPod in an effort to block out her sister Michelle, who was going on and on about the half marathon she was planning to run in September. She had placed fifth last year and said that she was aiming to be in the top three this time. There was nothing worse for Rica than listening to someone talking about their speed record when her own claim to athletic fame was receiving a "Participant" ribbon from the cross country run that her entire class had entered.

Her father steered the van around a sharp corner, causing something to crash behind her seat. Rica turned and saw that the camp stove had fallen from its perch on top of the sleeping bags. It now appeared to be in a better position, wedged between the second seat and the pillows.

"What was that?" her mother asked, frowning back from the front seat.

"Rica probably dropped something," Michelle suggested, without turning back to look.

"Oh, it was nothing," Rica answered. She noticed that her oldest sister, Petra, who was eighteen, gorgeous, and completely self-absorbed, hadn't even woken up despite the crashing and the talking. Petra had learned to tune out anything that didn't relate specifically to her, and Rica fell into this category. As the youngest of the three girls, Rica was always thought of as a child. But as much as she resented this fact, Rica could understand why. Her sisters' lives were filled with parties, friends with cars, and enough money from part-time jobs to do whatever they liked. Michelle had traveled out of town nine times this year for sporting competitions, and Petra had been on a three-month exchange to Switzerland. In contrast, Rica had less worldly interests. She generally stayed at home, enjoying the occasional Saturday night sleepover with the same friends she had known all her life. A "big night out" for Rica usually involved bowling and pizza, hardly something that she could expect Petra or Michelle to appreciate. Even Rica had to admit sometimes that her life was a bore.

Rica adjusted her earphones, turned up the music again, and closed her eyes.

It was summer vacation, and Rica and her family were about to spend it the way they spent every summer vacation – camping. Her mother had promised that this year would be more fun because they were vacationing with Aunt Joanne and Uncle Alan, who, along with her cousin Craig and his best friend, Finney, were going to camp on an adjoining site. "The more the merrier," her father had said. Rica could only hope.

When she felt the van slowing down, she opened her eyes and saw that they were pulling into a restaurant and gas station – again!

"Didn't you just get gas?" Rica complained.

"Nature calls!" her father replied cheerfully. She shook her head. *The man must have a bladder the size of a grape,* she thought.

"Are we there?" Petra asked, yawning and stretching as she opened her eyes and squinted out the side window. "Oh. Bathroom break?"

"And ice cream break," her mother suggested. "They have cones here. Does anybody want one?"

Petra looked as though someone had suggested that she eat dirt. "I'll go in and look around," she said. "But I don't want anything to eat. I can't afford to gain one more pound." She patted her flat stomach and sighed.

Michelle turned in her seat and rolled her eyes at Rica. "Olive Oyl doesn't want to get fat."

"What about you, Baby?" Rica heard her mother ask. "Do you want a cone?"

Rica cringed at the pet name and thought that it was no wonder why her sisters both thought of her as a child. She shook her head. "I just want to get moving. All these stops make the trip seem twice as long. If Dad drove any slower, we'd be better off just getting out and walking."

"Well, I'm going in," Michelle said, sliding the door open beside her.

Rica heard a vehicle pull up behind their van and the tent-trailer they were towing. It was her Uncle Alan, turning off the road so that he could keep following them. Unlike her father who could probably drive to Blackstone Park with a blindfold on, Uncle Alan wasn't sure of the way. Knowing that they would be parked for a few minutes, Rica closed her eyes and enjoyed the feeling of the hot sun beating through the glass next to her.

A sudden smack on the window beside her made her jolt sideways in her seat.

"Jeez, Craig!" Rica shrieked at her cousin. At seventeen, he was older than Rica, but he acted younger – much younger. His face was pressed sideways against her window, his nose flattened, his lips distorted, his cheeks spread out, his hands outstretched on either side of his face. He looked like a bug squashed on the windshield.

"Nice," she assured him, straightening up in her seat and shaking her head at his juvenile behavior. "You're hilarious. I guess that's why the girls at school love you so much."

Finney stood nearby laughing as Craig pulled himself away from the window. "Look what you did to the glass," Finney said, pointing at the smudges left behind.

"Great!" Rica called after them as they started into the store. "I get to look at your sweaty face print all the way to the park!"

The midday sun started to feel less enjoyable to her as the air conditioning dissipated from the vehicle. After ten minutes in the heat, she was starting to feel faint.

"Come on, come on," Rica said under her breath, watching the door to the restaurant. "How long can it take to grab an ice cream?"

She was undoing her seat belt and preparing to get out of the van when her family finally came trickling out of the store. Her mother and Aunt Joanne were talking, as usual. They never seemed to run out of things to say to each other, which was something that Rica couldn't understand. She never had much to say to Michelle or Petra.

It took five minutes for everyone to clamber back into the van, and another five minutes after that before the air conditioning felt comfortable again.

"It's so hot," Rica complained. "I don't see why Michelle and Petra get to sleep in the pup tent when we get there and I have to share the stuffy tent-trailer with you and Mom." It was an old argument, and one she knew she couldn't win.

"We have seniority," Michelle smirked.

"Hey, we would be lucky to have hot weather like this for the next two weeks," her father retorted. "Never complain about the sunshine, kiddo, or you'll bring on the rain."

It was one of her father's "wise and wonderful" sayings. He meant well, but he was like a walking, talking relic from the 1950's. All he needed were polyester pants. Rica closed her eyes and slumped down in her seat. Two more endless hours in the car stretched in front of her.

"We need a little music," she heard her father say.

Here it comes, she groaned to herself as she heard a CD case opening. A moment later, the CD player sucked in the disc, hesitated as if it knew the torture it was about to inflict, then let loose with the first painful chords of Waylon Jennings. Old-time country music now drowned out the sound of her iPod. *Could it get any worse?*

Her mother started to sing. Loudly. Rica opened her eyes and looked anxiously out the van window for a distraction. Her mind was spinning. There had to be a way to make this interminable trip bearable.

"Pull over!" she said suddenly, snapping up in her seat.

"Why? Did you see something?" her mother said, looking out the window.

"Just pull over, would you, Dad? Sorry, I didn't mean to scare you."

He slowed down and pulled over to the side of the road. Rica turned and saw her uncle pull up behind their trailer as she knew he would.

"I want to ride with them," she said. "I'll send Aunt Joanne up to ride with you guys."

"You're going to spend two hours in a car with Craig and Finney?" Petra asked with bored amusement.

"Is it something we said?" her father joked. "Is it my deodorant? I *think* I put it on this morning."

"I just need a change, that's all," Rica assured them, while Michelle rolled her eyes again.

"See you." Rica jumped out of the van and walked past her family's hard-top trailer to the passenger side of her uncle's SUV behind them. Joanne spoke with her for a moment and then gave up her seat and joined the front vehicle.

"There!" Rica said triumphantly, as she settled into the front passenger seat of the SUV and fastened her safety belt.

"Did you miss us or something?" Finney asked her.

"Yeah, that's it," she agreed sarcastically, and then sighed with self-satisfaction as her uncle pulled out to follow her parents' van.

Changing vehicles may not be much, Rica thought, *but it is a symbolic first step to changing everything about this vacation. I'll make this camping holiday unlike any other,* she swore to herself, *if it's the last thing I do.*

Chapter 2

Once at the campsite, it didn't take long for Michelle and Petra to slip into their usual vacation routines. Michelle disappeared as soon as they were finished setting up camp, and by the end of the next day she was already talking about how many boys she had met and how she had plans to go boating with a couple of them. Petra had spent her first day lying by herself at the end of the beach, book in hand, making no effort to meet anyone but managing to attract the attention of every male who walked past her.

Rica lay despondently on her beach towel on the second day of the vacation and realized that she too had fallen into her usual routine –

sitting on the beach with her parents like an overprotected child.

"You're not falling asleep there, are you?" her mother asked as she walked back up the beach from the lake, shaking the water from her shoulder-length hair. She laid a brightly striped towel down on the sand beside Rica. "You don't want to get sunstroke."

"No, I'm just lying here. Bored." Rica sat up, found the elastic she had left on her towel, pulled her thick, sandy hair up into a loose ponytail, and then picked up her sunglasses.

"Look out!" a voice suddenly called out in warning. Rica turned toward the voice, squinting into the sun. A perfectly timed volleyball smacked her in the center of her forehead.

"Oh, wow! Sorry!" She heard the concerned voice before her eyes could come back into focus. A moment later, a hand grabbed her arm. "Are you okay?"

Rica rubbed her head and nodded, wondering if she'd have a welt on her face later. *That would be perfect*, she thought. *I'm not just a short, dorky girl, but a short, dorky girl with a swollen forehead. What could be worse?*

"Oh, Baby! Are you all right?" Her mother was calling her "baby" in front of someone who sounded young and male. *What have I done to deserve this?* she thought.

"My buddy can really spike a ball hard. Trouble is, he can't aim!" said the voice. Rica shielded her eyes against the sun so that she could see the person who was bending down to pick up the ball from the sand beside her.

There was a catch in her throat as she found herself looking into a pair of clear blue eyes. Smooth face, tanned skin, blond hair with a bit of a curl. Maybe sixteen or seventeen years old. *Oh my God,* she thought. *He's gorgeous!*

"Anyway, sorry," he said as he picked up the ball and ran back down the beach to the volleyball net. An assortment of people had gathered on the sand to play. A couple of them waved to her with sympathetic looks on their faces before they turned and resumed the game.

Rica stared in the direction of the volleyball players with her mouth slightly ajar.

"Hey," her mother said, poking Rica's arm. "I can see that being hit with the ball couldn't have hurt too much. Why don't you go and join them? You could make some new friends," she suggested.

Every year for as long as Rica could remember, it was always the same. If someone floated by on a raft, her mother would suggest that Rica paddle out too. Baseball? "Go on, Rica, just stand in the outfield at least." Soccer? "Just run out there on the field, Sweetie, and someone will kick the ball to you." She never seemed to tire of pushing her daughter to get involved and make friends. Now it was, "Go and play volleyball."

"I'm fine." Rica said, and pulled her knees up to her chest, tightening her arms around them and looking at her toes. The second toe on each foot was longer than her big toe. "A sign of intelligence," her father told her once.

"Okay, but it's your loss. He's pretty cute," her mother said, nodding toward the boy as he tossed the ball to someone on the opposite team.

"Jeez, Mom!" Rica couldn't believe it. She was a mother. She shouldn't be thinking of that stuff.

Rica's mother looked younger than her forty years. Her long legs and tight muscle tone made her look fantastic in her two-piece bathing suit. Rica didn't mind when people told her how pretty her mother was, but she hated it when they finished by saying, "You're just like your father."

Rica looked down the beach to where her

father was playing Frisbee with Craig and Finney. Compared to the boys, her father appeared short, stocky, and uncoordinated. His stomach bulged slightly over the elastic waist of his knee-length swim trunks. She watched as he lunged for the Frisbee, falling into the sand after missing by several inches. He laughed as he stood up and brushed at the sand that clung to the sweat-dampened areas of his body. He was only five foot five, shorter than Rica's mother and older sisters. Rica was the only one in the family still shorter than her father. She loved her dad, but she didn't want to be built like him.

Craig and Finney were both in great shape. They played on the same hockey and soccer teams every year and competed in track and field. As much as she hated to admit it, they were both pretty talented sports players.

She shook her head as she saw Finney dive for the Frisbee and land in a cloud of sand. He held the plastic disk triumphantly in the air. Finney was competitive, even when playing a friendly game of Frisbee.

"Your point!" she heard someone yell by the volleyball net. She slipped her sunglasses on and watched the volleyball players for another few minutes. *Sweat can look really good on the right bodies,* she thought appreciatively.

"Rica! Coming in?" she heard from the water. Her father was standing in the lake, water to his knees, gesturing for her to join him. Rica thought for a second, then stood up.

"I'm going for a swim with Dad," she said to her mother, who had placed a straw hat over her face to keep the sun from her eyes.

"Good for you!" her mother answered from beneath the hat.

Rica straightened up and wrapped her towel around her waist for the walk to the water's edge. No use exposing her body to scrutiny any longer than she had to.

From the corner of her eye, she could see the volleyball players on her left. She sucked in her stomach, felt her chest expand, and walked stiffly across the hot sand, hoping she wasn't wincing with each burning step. *Look cool,* she told herself. *Air into the chest, not the stomach. Think tall.*

The dampness of the cool, hard sand by the water's edge was a welcome relief. She loosened her towel and dropped it onto the dry sand behind her, then tossed her sunglasses onto it. Stepping over the small ridge of washed up weeds that lined the edge of the lake, she felt the cold waters of Upper Blackstone lap over her feet. Goose bumps immediately covered her body and she instinctively hugged herself.

"It's nice and warm!" her father called out to her.

"That's what you always say!" she called back. She inched forward, taking small steps until there was no avoiding the water hitting the bottom of her swimsuit.

"Chicken!" her father yelled to her.

She was just about to answer when she heard someone yell *"Chaaaarge!"* followed by the pounding of feet down the beach and the splashing of legs through the water. She turned just in time to see Craig and Finney heaving toward her, one on each side, as they ran past and dove into the water, leaving her soaked from their deliberate attack.

"Craig!" she shrieked, stepping backward clumsily into shallower water.

She heard laughter and looked over her shoulder to see her volleyball player and a couple of his friends looking in her direction from their court up on the beach. She felt herself flush despite the cool temperature of the lake. Turning back toward the open water where Craig and Finney had just joined her father, she stepped forward and dove as gracefully as she could, swimming several strokes under water and then coming up a few feet ahead. She concentrated on performing clean strokes – thanks to Mrs. Henderson, her swim instructor for six months when she was eight – until she reached the red, floating markers.

"You guys are going down!" she threatened.

Craig pushed away from her on his back and kicked his feet, sending a spray into her face. Finney was grinning at her as he swayed in the waves and hung onto the roped marker. She scowled at him, and he responded by raising his feet and joining Craig in the splashing assault.

"Funny," she said, swimming a few feet away from them and diving under the rope. She came up beside her father.

"Uncle Casey," Craig called to her father, "you'd better move or you might get splashed."

Her father laughed and turned his feet toward the boys. "I'm already wet, guys. I can take you!" He started kicking as hard as he could, sending a fountain of water toward them. Rica laughed and turned onto her back, joining her father in a two-on-two battle that lasted until her father started to gasp and it appeared as if he couldn't hold himself up any longer. While the boys kept on kicking, Rica swam toward shore.

Floating, Rica glanced to her left and noticed the blue-eyed volleyball player, who was now wading into the water with his friends. She thought he might be watching her and, despite the cool water, her face flushed again. The boy was just too cute.

Maybe there is hope for this vacation after all. Perhaps the answer to her boring family vacation was standing right there, getting ready to dive under the cool waves washing in from a passing ski boat.

"Hey, it's Michelle!" her father called to her, walking toward shore and pointing at the skier passing behind a large motorboat.

Rica turned and saw Michelle skim easily across the wake of the boat and then lean left to cross back to the other side. Michelle signaled the driver, who then circled past the dock at the end of the beach, allowing Michelle to glide straight to the end of the dock and come to a perfect stop within feet of the ladder.

"You should learn how to ski, Rica," her father said loudly enough for everyone on the beach to hear. "You've got sturdy legs, and you're short enough that you wouldn't have far to fall."

Rica groaned and looked back anxiously at her volleyball player, but it didn't seem as if he was paying attention to her any longer. He was too busy staring at Petra, who had just arrived on the beach dressed in her red bikini with small ties at the hips that accentuated her perfect figure. She walked to a quiet spot away from the family and unrolled her beach mat, then sat down and started spreading sun tan lotion onto her lithe legs.

The volleyball players appeared to have forgotten all about Rica. With their backs turned toward her, she decided it was as good a time as any to walk out of the lake unobserved and get a towel to wrap around herself.

"Frisbee, Rica?" her father called to her from the beach as she reached down quickly for her towel.

Not Frisbee, she thought. *Not with my father and not where anyone can see how bad I am at it. I need to do something really cool to impress this guy. Something he'll never forget. Something. Anything!*

And with that, she felt a buzzing in her ears and her head started to spin. She dropped to the sand in a dead faint.

Chapter 3

"Is she okay?"

A male voice cut through the darkness, and Rica tried to remember where she was.

"Rica? Someone put some more water on her face," she heard her mother saying. Something cool and damp wiped her forehead. She opened her eyes and looked up at a sea of blurred faces bent over her own. Mom. Dad. Craig. Finney.

"Here," her father was saying. "Have a drink." She let him tip a water bottle up to her lips, and she took a sip gratefully.

"She's prone to sunstroke," her mother was telling everyone.

"I'm fine," Rica said, pushing herself up

slowly from the sand. Her father held her arm and supported her as she sat up. She was stunned to see that the cute volleyball player was there, by her feet, bent over her stubby, sand-covered legs.

"She hasn't eaten today and she's had too much sun," her mother explained to the strangers who had gathered around them.

"I just got dizzy from bending over too fast. I'm fine," Rica insisted. She looked for her towel so that she could cover herself, but someone had used it to soak water from the lake for her forehead. She grabbed her father's arm and pulled herself up to her feet.

"What happened?" Michelle asked, running up to the cluster of people and pushing past to stand next to the volleyball player.

"She fainted," Craig said mockingly. "Dropped like a stone. One minute she's standing, the next minute she's doing a face plant into the sand."

"Rica, Rica, Rica," Michelle said in a way that made Rica feel like a total screw-up once again.

"Come on, Baby. We'll take you into the shade." Her mother was reaching for her other arm, and she knew she was about to be escorted across the sand like a helpless child. She was thinking about shaking her parents off and saying that she was perfectly capable of walking on her own, when she heard *his* voice from behind her.

"Here. I'll help." He took Rica by the elbow, and her mother miraculously fell behind to follow. Rica couldn't believe her luck. Deciding that perhaps she *was* still a bit dizzy, she leaned in toward the tall, well-built body, using his strong arm for support.

"Are you all right?" he asked with concern, looking down at her with caring eyes that made her legs feel weak again – but for different reasons this time.

"Much better now that you're here," she quipped flirtatiously, and then blushed at her boldness. He grinned and laughed.

When they got to the top of the beach, her mother reached down and took her own towel from the sand, laying it beneath the trees that lined the grassy park behind. The volleyball player escorted Rica over and helped lower her into the shade.

"Thanks," she said, smiling up at him.

"No problem. Sorry you aren't feeling well." He smiled back and held out her sunglasses. "These were beside your towel down at the water. They're yours, right?"

"Yeah, thanks." She put them on and then realized she didn't need them in the shade. She tipped them up onto the top of her head.

"I'm Rica," she told him.

"I know. I heard your mother saying ..."

Out of nowhere, Rica then heard, "And I'm Michelle. Rica's my little sister." *Only one year younger,* Rica thought resentfully. *One year younger, one bra size smaller, and one foot shorter.*

Michelle stood confidently in her bathing suit, her face glowing and radiant. She didn't even need make-up. Rica was sure that her own complexion was dreadfully pale after the fainting episode.

"I'm Stefan," he said to Rica and Michelle. "And that's my buddy Kyle down there talking to your brother."

Michelle and Rica answered, "Cousin – he's our cousin," in unison, dismayed by the thought that Craig could be considered their brother.

"And that's our other sister," Michelle went on, waving a hand dismissively toward Petra, who was busy asking her parents what had happened. "She's a bit of a girly girl. I'm more into sports."

"Yeah, I saw you skiing," Stefan said appreciatively. "You're pretty good."

"How are you, Baby?" her mother interrupted as she came over with a sliced orange and a bottle of water. "Here, have this. You probably need to be hydrated."

"I should go," Stefan said, indicating that Kyle was waiting for him down on the beach.

Rica started to thank him, but was cut off by Michelle. "Thank you for helping us out." Michelle was touching his arm, Rica noticed. "I guess my little sister just can't handle the sun."

"Hey, I'm right here," Rica protested. "Don't talk about me like I'm invisible. And I can so handle the sun. I just bent down too fast."

Stefan looked slightly embarrassed by their exchange as he turned to leave. "Maybe we'll see you around," he said over his shoulder.

"We could go skiing sometime," Michelle suggested.

"Thanks again for helping," Rica called after him. If nothing else, she had the last word with him. They both watched as he walked across the sand to join Kyle.

When the boys had walked down the

beach and were no longer in view, Michelle stopped staring and started stretching.

"I have to go train," Michelle said, swinging her arms in a loosening motion. Michelle normally ran for an hour a day when they were at home. With only a month to go before her half marathon, Michelle had told everyone that she would be running ten miles every day during the vacation.

"Isn't it way too hot to go running?" Rica asked. "Why don't you do it in the evening when it's cooler?"

"That's why you're not an athlete, Rica," Michelle told her condescendingly. "You just don't like to push yourself."

I'd like to push you, Rica thought. She watched as Michelle walked back over to join her parents, as well as Alan and Joanne who had just come from their campsite with their chairs and cooler. Michelle took her T-shirt and shorts from a nearby tote bag and pulled them on over her bathing suit.

"I have to go and get my sneakers and then I'm off for my run," Michelle said as she slipped into her flip flops for the walk back to the site. "I'll see you later."

"Take lots of water with you," her mother

called after her.

Rica watched as Michelle headed across the grass toward the campground.

"So. Want me to spread some sunblock on your back for you?" Finney asked as he dropped onto the sand next to Rica.

Rica was pretty sure that Finney was aware of every muscle in his body as he leaned back on his elbow. She tried to judge what she would think of him if she didn't already know him, and decided that although he had a pretty decent body and a not unpleasant face, his taste in bathing suits was all wrong. He was wearing a long, loose pair of bright, floral shorts that made him look as if he was a surfer wannabe. They slipped too low on his narrow hips.

"Sunblock? Duh! I'm in the shade," she told him, wondering why she had to explain the obvious. She wondered if her mother had heard his offer to apply lotion to her back. It would be embarrassing to have a boy rubbing her back in front of her parents, even if it was just her cousin's friend.

Rica stood and, satisfied that she was no longer dizzy, took her mother's towel. "I think I'll go for a walk," she said, ignoring Finney's look of disappointment.

"Oh, that doesn't sound very wise," her mother said worriedly. She turned to Joanne and Alan. "You missed the excitement. She passed out, right down there on the beach. Too much sun."

"I'm *fine,*" Rica told them before they could even ask. "I'm just going for a walk, not a marathon run like some people."

"I'll come with you if you want," Finney suggested.

"No thanks. I just want to be by myself." She pulled on a T-shirt and picked up her sandals before starting down the beach. She had watched Stefan head the same way with his friend. If she was lucky, she might run into him.

She had noticed how interested he seemed when Michelle had mentioned that she was an athlete. He obviously liked sports, but Rica would never be able to compete that way against Michelle. If she wanted to get his attention, she'd have to find another way.

Maybe there's a different kind of game to play, she thought, *one that puts me on an even playing field with my sisters.* She smiled at her own audacity.

Chapter 4

About an hour later, Rica had almost forgotten why she was walking along the winding roads at all, when she realized that Stefan and Kyle were sitting at a campsite directly in front of her.

"Oh, hi," Stefan said, turning toward Rica and looking surprised to see her. "Are you visiting someone over this way?"

Her face turned red and she fumbled for an explanation. "Uh, not really. I mean ... I was just going for a walk."

She was standing awkwardly, wondering why she hadn't put her shorts on – she felt odd in her bathing suit and T-shirt now that she wasn't on the beach. She pulled at the hem of her shirt, stretching the sides down a bit.

"We were just heading into town," Stefan said, nodding toward a black Sunfire parked next to them. "Do you want to come?"

"Is that your car?" she asked, wondering how old he must be if he owned a car.

"It's mine," Kyle answered proudly.

Rica looked at their site, taking note of the single pup tent and two lawn chairs.

"Are you guys here by yourselves?"

"Yeah. We're male bonding," Kyle answered, and the two of them laughed comfortably together.

"We won't be in town for long. We just have to pick up a couple of things," Stefan promised. "Why don't you come along?"

"Okay," Rica said shyly. "Can I run back to our site and change first?"

"We'll drive you," Kyle offered. "Come on."

She hesitated for a minute, but then hopped into the back seat of the car and thought how this vacation was finally shaping up to be better than any other. The two boys got in the front. Kyle started the engine and the car roared. "Dual tailpipes," he bragged. They pulled out of the site and she directed them to number 312.

The campsite looked deserted. "Everyone

still at the beach?" Stefan asked.

"I guess so. I'll just be a second." She jumped out of the car. Kyle left the engine running. Passing the pup tent that Michelle and Petra shared and climbing into the tent-trailer that she shared with her parents, Rica tossed through the few clothes she had packed. She quickly chose her tan capris and a black tank top. She pulled both over her bathing suit and was about to step out of the trailer when she caught sight of herself in the small mirror that her mother kept hanging by her bed.

"Oh my God," she groaned, and grabbed a hairbrush. She pulled it through her tangled hair hurriedly and then quickly applied some of her mother's mascara and blush. "Good as it gets," she muttered to herself, climbing out and zipping the tent closed behind her.

In the back of her mind, Rica knew that she should be asking Kyle to take her to the beach first so that she could get permission to go for a ride. The problem was that her parents would never agree to let her go into town in a car with two boys. She didn't care. She decided that even though it was wrong, she was going to put "Operation Exciting Vacation" ahead of being the good girl. *Good girls are dull girls*, she thought.

"All set," she announced as she climbed back into the car. Stefan turned to smile at her and she wondered how he got his teeth so white.

The fifteen-minute drive into Northbrook was made to the full-volume accompaniment of an old Eminem CD. Rica's ears throbbed along to the music, but she was relieved not to have to make small talk. Both of the front windows were open all the way. Even though her hair was tied back, the wind was whipping loose tendrils across her face.

The car slowed down by the edge of town and pulled into the gravel lot of the general store. As they were climbing out of the car, Rica caught Kyle looking at her hair in the rearview mirror. She put her hands up and could feel that the mass of frizzy curls had gotten out of control. *Perfect,* she groaned to herself as she tried to flatten her hair behind her ears.

She followed the boys into the store and surveyed the rows of items for sale: groceries, the usual array of plastic pails and shovels for the beach, rubber boots, fishing gear, and tacky T-shirts with Blackstone Lake imprinted across the body of a trout on the back.

"What are you buying?" she asked, following Stefan down the food aisle.

"Just some staples," he answered, reaching for a loaf of bread. His arm brushed against hers and it made her feel warm. "Some beans. Eggs. Beer."

"Beer?" Rica asked loudly. He looked past her, his brows knit together, and then met her eyes and shook his head in warning. She looked back toward the front of the store and saw the old man who had been working the counter every summer that she could remember. He was looking back at them suspiciously.

"How old are you?" she whispered to Stefan.

"Sixteen. Kyle's seventeen. He looks older so he's going to buy it. Maybe you shouldn't have come in. You look too young. How old are you, anyway?" he asked, looking carefully at her worried face.

"Older than I look," she lied.

"Go back out to the car," he advised. He reached over and tucked a loose strand of hair behind her ear. "Go on, before you get us all in trouble."

She looked at him for a moment and then decided to do as he suggested. She'd rather be in the car if they were doing something illegal than be standing beside them like an accomplice. The bell above the door announced her departure. She could feel the eyes of the old man burning into the back of her head as she left.

She sat restlessly in the hot car for what seemed like hours, before the two boys came out carrying bags of groceries.

Kyle opened the car door and passed the groceries to Rica in the back seat. "He wouldn't sell us the beer," Kyle said with disgust. "Asked me for ID as soon as I started picking up a case." He and Stefan climbed into the car, and Kyle started the engine.

"Just pull over there," Stefan said, pointing to the side of the store that had no windows.

Kyle nodded, drove out, and then backed in at the side. "We shouldn't have to wait long," he said.

"For what?" Rica asked.

"For that," Stefan answered, pointing at a car pulling in with a man behind the wheel. Stefan got out of the car and called across to the man as he headed for the door of the general store.

They chatted for a moment, and Rica saw the older man shake his head and walk by

Stefan to go into the store.

"No luck," Stefan said with disappointment when he returned.

"You try the next one," Stefan said to Kyle.

They waited ten minutes before another car pulled up. A girl in her early twenties got out. Kyle met her at the corner of the building. They spoke for a minute, and then Rica watched as Kyle gave her some money and she went into the store. He got back into the car and high-fived Stefan.

"Way to go, Buddy," Stefan said with admiration.

"It's costing us though," Kyle warned. "She said we had to pay for a six-pack for her."

"It's worth it," Stefan said with a shrug. "At least we're getting the brew, right?" He turned around and winked at Rica.

Rica nodded and then looked out the window. If her parents ever found out about this, they'd have a fit.

The girl came back out of the store with a case of twenty-four. Kyle got out of the car and opened the trunk. He then took the case from her and placed it inside. "I could only carry one at a time," the girl said. "I'll go back in for the other."

Rica's mouth dropped open.

"You're getting two cases?" she asked Stefan, trying to keep her voice light.

"We're camping for a week," Stefan explained. Rica wondered how they would ever finish it all.

The girl was heading back toward them again. Kyle took the second case from her eagerly. He thanked her and got back into the car.

"She has to go back in for the six-pack now. That guy is going to think she's a heavy drinker."

They pulled out of the parking lot and sped back toward the park. Rica wondered if her parents had noticed her absence yet. She suspected that she had been gone almost an hour already. Kyle had slipped in an old CD of a Queen concert and had it blasting as he sang along loudly.

"I like these guys," Rica yelled from the back seat. She tried not to feel self-conscious as the boys sang along to "Fat-Bottomed Girls."

Rica gazed out the window and caught sight of someone ahead on the road. It was Michelle and she was running along the asphalt, her stride steady and strong, muscles toned. Her hair was tied back and swinging rhythmically with her pace. She must have heard the car approaching because she moved cautiously to the shoulder of the road.

"Hey, isn't that your sister?" Stefan asked, looking in the side mirror after they passed the runner.

"It could be," Rica said, looking back as though she hadn't really considered it. "Hard to say," she concluded, facing forward.

"I'll stop and see if she wants a lift," Kyle said.

"Oh, she won't," Rica assured him. "She's in training. She won't even consider cutting her run short. Just keep going." Rica saw Kyle looking at her skeptically in the rearview mirror. "Go on," she said to the questioning eyes. "Keep going."

"We can at least give her the option," Kyle said. He pulled the car safely onto the sandy shoulder and waited for the girl to approach.

Rica slid down in the back seat and wished she could disappear.

"Hi. Michelle, right?" Kyle said out his window as she started to pass the car.

Michelle slowed and then stopped, smiling at the two boys as she recognized who they were.

"Yeah, hi again," she said, looking across the car at Stefan, who sat grinning at her from the passenger seat. And then her eyes fell into the back seat and she gripped the edge of the driver's door and leaned down. "Well, well! You have little Rica with you. Where were *you*?"

Rica shrugged as though it was no big deal. "We just went into town. For a ride."

"That's *great*. Did you have fun?" She was smiling, but Rica recognized the edge to the smile. Michelle knew Rica would never have been allowed to go anywhere in a car with two older boys.

"Do you want a ride?" Kyle asked. "We're heading back."

Say no, Rica thought.

"That would be nice," Michelle said sweetly. Rica felt her heart sink. Michelle crossed behind the car and climbed into the seat behind Stefan. "I hope you don't mind if I sweat in your car," she apologized. "I've been running for an hour and a half, and it's so hot today."

"I told you it was too hot," Rica said. She hoped that Stefan would see how foolish her sister was for running in the middle of the afternoon on a hot August day.

"Wow," Stefan said admiringly. "An hour and a half. You must be in amazing condition." He turned in his seat to get a better look at her.

Michelle took a drink from her water bottle and then squirted a bit down the front of her shirt, causing it to cling even more closely than it had with the sweat. "I do it all the time," she assured him. "I'm training."

"That's what Rica was telling us. She was pretty sure you wouldn't want a ride."

"Is that right?" Michelle looked across the seat and smiled broadly at her sister. "Well, I guess I surprised you, didn't I, Rica?"

The car approached the entrance to the park. Kyle waved his pass at the attendant as they went through the gate. The narrow road wound through trees for a mile before smaller dirt roads split off and led into camping areas.

"What are you guys doing tonight?" Stefan asked.

"Not much. What do you have in mind?" Michelle asked, holding the back of his seat as she leaned in toward him.

"Baseball," he suggested. "There's a ball diamond near your campsite and I hear they have games most nights."

"You know where our site is?" She looked at Rica again with eyebrows raised. "That's super. I'd love to play ball. Rica doesn't play baseball though. Right, Rica?"

Visions of baseball games of the past flashed through Rica's mind. Missing fly balls. Tripping over the bag at third. She knew that Michelle expected her to say no.

"Sure, I'll play," Rica said with as much confidence as she could muster.

"Super," Michelle said, looking as though she was holding back a laugh.

Before Kyle could turn on their camp road, Rica leaned forward and asked him to let them out. "No use driving all the way around the circle," she said. "We can walk the last bit."

Kyle pulled the car over. "If you want to come over for a beer after we play ball, we've got it covered," he offered. "We just picked some up in town."

"Really?" Michelle answered, her face barely able to contain the pleasure she was deriving from this entire conversation. "You bought beer while you were in town with Rica? That's cool. We'll see you later on."

The girls got out of the car. Kyle drove off and dust from the dry soil of the dirt road rose behind the car. They walked down the road together, Michelle humming merrily to herself.

"Had to get out at the end of the road, huh, Rica? So I guess Mom and Dad didn't know you were out for a car ride, doing your booze shopping. You are in *so* much trouble," Michelle said with scarcely veiled pleasure.

"Hey, where have you girls been?" their parents called from Alan and Joanne's site as the two girls walked up the road.

"Don't you dare tell them!" Rica warned Michelle under her breath. "I didn't do anything wrong. I just went for the ride, that's all. I didn't even know what they were going to buy."

"You shouldn't even have gone for the ride," Michelle hissed. "Mom would freak if she knew." She grabbed her sister's arm and leaned in so that no one else would hear. "I'll tell you what. I wouldn't mind having a little fun of my own this week. I'll consider not telling Mom and Dad what you did today if you promise to back me up later. Deal?"

Rica thought for a second before biting her lip and nodding.

They turned in at the campsite and joined everyone where they sat with their lawn chairs circled around an unlit fire pit.

"We were just walking," Michelle said innocently. "I thought it was about time that Rica and I did something together, and it was fun. Isn't that right, Rica?" She squeezed Rica's arm as they walked toward the group.

"Uh-huh," Rica agreed weakly.

Michelle leaned in close to Rica as they approached the campsite. "I may still decide to tell them," she warned in a whisper. "So you'd better not forget that you owe me big time."

Rica took a deep breath and smiled at her parents. She had gotten away with this one, she thought to herself, but Michelle would never let her forget it. And to make things even worse, she had promised the boys she would play baseball! She was a *terrible* baseball player. This could turn into the most embarrassing night of her life. And the boys were expecting them to go over and drink afterward! If she didn't go, Rica would look like a baby, and Michelle would have Stefan all to herself.

Rica sat down on the picnic table beside Finney and put her head down on the table with a groan.

"Still feeling sick?" Finney asked her.

"You have no idea," she replied.

Chapter 5

By six o'clock that night, the sky had started to cloud over, and the air was getting cool in the tree-shaded campsite. By suppertime, everyone had changed into sweatshirts and jeans.

"I'm going to the ballpark after supper," Michelle told her parents.

"Why don't we all go?" her father asked. "I haven't played ball yet this year. I'll take you all on."

"Good idea," her mother agreed. "It's supposed to rain tomorrow, so we might as well do what we can while the weather is good." She rose from the picnic table and picked up her empty plate, kissing her husband, who was seated, on the top of his head.

"Whose turn to do dishes tonight?"

"I'll do them," Rica offered quickly. "You guys can go ahead."

Michelle looked at her with feigned disappointment. "You decided not to play?"

"I just thought I'd help out here," Rica said. "I'll meet you at the park later."

"That's nice of you, Sweetie," her mother said, appearing oblivious to the girls' strained interaction. "Okay, baseball it is."

"I'll come, but I won't play," Petra said, closing the cover of her latest romance novel. "I'm finished with this one if anyone wants to borrow it."

"You're joking, right?" her father asked as he finished the last of his food. He rose from the table and went to the van. He dug out a couple of ball gloves and a softball and bat from under the front seats.

Rica scraped their supper remnants into the garbage bag they kept next to the picnic table and watched as the rest of her family headed next door to Alan and Joanne's site. Everyone there was easily convinced to join the game. She could hear Craig and Finney boasting that they could hit the ball past the end of the field, across the road, and into the trees behind the children's playground. She wondered how Craig and Michelle had managed to get an overabundance of athletic genes, and how she had managed to be born with none.

Working at a snail's pace, Rica took twenty minutes to wash the dishes outside in the plastic dishpan and to dry them before storing them in the trailer. When she had cleaned up all that she could, she headed down the narrow camp road. *There's no avoiding it,* she thought as she approached the field. *I'm going to have to play baseball.*

There was a picnic table at the edge of the clearing that provided an open view of the ball diamond. Rica hesitated for only a moment before deciding to sit down to watch the game from there. If she was lucky, no one would insist that she play. She climbed onto the tabletop and hunched forward, putting her feet onto the bench.

There were about fifteen people on the field, half of them her family. Her father was pitching, Alan was third baseman, and Joanne was shortstop. Petra sat on the bench behind the first base line, quietly encouraging whoever was hitting. Stefan was in center field, waiting for the next hit.

"Rica!" Finney called out loudly as he picked up the bat and walked toward home plate. "Come join us!"

His shout caused Stefan to turn and look at Rica across the field. He waved and smiled at her before turning back. Her heart skipped a beat. *He noticed I'm here,* she sang to herself, feeling ridiculously pleased by his smile. Rica felt energized enough by the attention to wave brightly to Michelle, who stood scowling back at her from her position on first base.

It was getting too cold to be sitting still. Rica pulled the sleeves of her sweatshirt down over her hands to keep warm.

Finney was ready to bat and everyone moved back as far as they could. Stefan moved back and crossed the road toward Rica's clearing, anticipating a long hit. He leaned his upper body forward on his knees, swaying slightly, looking ready for the batter. Finney dug his shoes into the dirt and got in position over the plate. His bat was twitching as if it was eager for contact. Rica saw Stefan look toward her. The determination on Finney's face increased. He crouched and was poised as if he was preparing for a Major League pitch.

"He can't hit it!" Michelle was calling.

"Come on, Dad. You can do it!"

Her father leaned back in his best imitation of a Major League pitcher and then brought his arm around, releasing the ball with the greatest speed he could. Despite the pitch being wide and outside, Finney leaned forward and swung. The bat made contact with a crack that echoed across the park. The ball spun low across the field and landed on the road, bouncing away from Stefan who was running across the gravel and lowering his glove. He dove forward onto the grass and snatched up the ball, leaped to his feet and flung it forward to the shortstop, missing the glove. Finney had comfortably touched home plate before the ball was passed to the catcher. He high-fived the kid who had been on third and crossed home plate before him.

Stefan groaned and looked across the short distance to where Rica was watching him. His face indicated a hint of embarrassment at his inability to stop the run.

"Is that guy your cousin too?" Stefan asked, approaching Rica and sitting on the table next to her.

She shook her head. "No, that's my cousin's friend Finney. He takes himself pretty seriously."

Stefan wiped the hair back from his forehead. Rica noticed he was sweating slightly. She put her hands under her legs and rocked a bit, staring down at her dirty running shoes.

"Why aren't you playing?" he asked, looking at her quizzically.

She scrunched her face and decided to be honest. "I stink at baseball. I would look like an idiot out there."

He laughed. "No one cares. Heck, we're playing with all kinds of people. Not everyone is as good as Craig and his buddy."

Rica shrugged and watched her mother getting ready to bat.

"Your parents seem nice," Stefan said. "And your sisters."

"They're okay," she replied, watching her mother hit a grounder straight toward first. Craig got to the ball first, picked it up, and touched the base before tagging the runner for good measure. Her mother grabbed his hat in response and then ran around the bases with him chasing her as the others cheered her on.

"Do you want to go for a walk?" Stefan asked suddenly. Rica looked at him, his head tilted, his blue eyes looking into her eyes with eagerness.

"I guess so," she said, trying to sound casual. Inside, her heart was pounding, fireworks were exploding in her head, and she was having trouble breathing.

They walked up the hill away from the park, the voices of the ball players getting farther and farther away. They chatted easily as they headed along the paved road that led to the north beach. They circled the amphitheater where nature films were shown on Wednesdays.

Stefan told her he lived in the Midwest, that he was headed into the twelfth grade in September and hoped to make the volleyball team. He and his friend Kyle had come camping on their own while his parents were in Europe. He was enjoying himself, meeting lots of interesting people in the park. "Like you," he said, and she felt her ears turn red.

Rica decided to lie and told him that she was headed into eleventh grade, and then kicked herself when she realized that Michelle would probably tell him the same thing. She told him about living in a town of only five thousand people, and he laughed when she complained about how everyone in town knew when she was blowing her nose.

"And being the youngest in the family is the worst," she confided. "It's like they think they know what I'm going to do before I even do it."

"I'd think being the youngest is an advantage," he suggested. "Your sisters pave the way for you, breaking all the rules before you get stuck having to live by them."

"I suppose," she answered doubtfully. "What about you? Do you have brothers or sisters?"

"No, I'm the only one and it really puts the pressure on me. My mother is a minister, so she expects me to set a moral and ethical example."

"Do you?" she asked, thinking of the beer he and Kyle had bought.

"Not if I can help it." His grin was crooked, and she wondered what other kind of trouble he was prone to.

As they came out into the clearing at a small, empty beach, Stefan took her hand. Rica felt his warm fingers curl around hers and she wondered if her hands felt hot or cold to him. They sat down on a picnic table and looked across at the gray water as it blended with the cloudy sky.

"Are you warm enough?" he asked her.

She nodded, but he put his arm around her anyway and pulled her close so she could feel the warmth of him through their sweat-shirts. They sat like that for a few minutes, not speaking, lost in their thoughts until Stefan turned and put his finger against the side of Rica's chin, turning her face to his. She watched as he came closer. She saw his face tilt so their noses wouldn't crash, saw his eyes slowly close, felt his lips press against hers. It was only for a few seconds, and then it was over. He moved back, looking at her.

She was embarrassed to think that it was her first real kiss. She didn't count Vince Corrigan kissing her on the front porch when they were both six, or Matt Withers kissing her in the closet when they played "Spin the Bottle" when they were eleven.

This kiss was a real one, a boyfriend / girl-friend kind of kiss. It was entirely different. Stefan was still looking at her, as if he was wait-ing for a reaction or something, so she leaned forward and kissed him back, pressing her lips into his eagerly. He didn't exactly move away, but he shifted just enough to make the kiss softer, gentler, sweeter. Rica thought she would burst, she felt so good.

They sat together on the table for about half an hour, Rica leaning into his shoulder. Every now and again they would look at each other and kiss, extending each kiss for so long that she wondered if there was a world record for the longest kiss. She was beginning to think that she must be very good at this kissing thing, especially when Stefan looked so disappointed by her reluctant announcement that she should be getting back.

"I'd like to do this again," Stefan said to her as they strolled back across the amphitheater grounds.

"Me too," Rica agreed. She kissed him on the neck, and he gently placed his hands on her waist and pulled her close. After another long kiss, they kept walking.

The mosquitoes were getting aggressive by the time Rica got back to the campsite. Stefan had said good-bye and turned off onto the road toward his site, and she had walked the last few minutes by herself, swatting at her head when the persistent buzzing sounded too close to her ears. Even the threat of West Nile Virus wasn't going to ruin her night.

"Hey, there she is!" her father called as

she passed. She saw her family huddled by the campfire in the clearing of Alan and Joanne's site, and turned in to join them.

"Where did you go with Stefan?" Michelle asked, scowling at her from the other side of the fire pit.

"We just went for a walk. Checked out the north beach." Rica could feel everyone looking at her. *What? Could they tell she had been kissing Stefan for so long? Were her lips swollen or something?* Finney was staring straight at her. She stared back and made a face.

"Did you have fun?" her mother asked cannily, handing her a hot chocolate. Rica took the cup gratefully. Her hands were frozen.

"Yeah. We had a pretty good time," she answered casually, avoiding Michelle's eyes.

No baseball, no drinking, Rica thought to herself. *And I got myself a boyfriend, despite Michelle's flirting, so this vacation is looking a lot more interesting.*

She sipped her hot chocolate and glanced across at Michelle, who sat huddled in a lawn chair with a blanket wrapped around her shoulders. Michelle was glaring at her, the fire's flames reflecting in her eyes. Rica was reminded of the low-budget horror movies that she loved to watch. If this was a movie, Michelle would be the axe murderer. Rica looked away and shivered, but not from the cool night air. She could see that Michelle was furious, probably because her own plans for drinking with Stefan had been foiled. Michelle appeared poised for battle. If there was anything that Rica knew about her sister, it was that Michelle wasn't about to lose any competition without a fight.

As promising as this vacation was becoming, Rica could see that it was about to get even more interesting!

Chapter 6

The next day, the gentle rhythm of steady rainfall against the canvas of the trailer provided an excuse to lie in bed later than usual. Rica pulled her pillow closer and snuggled down into her sleeping bag, feeling the warmth of the flannel and falling contentedly back to sleep. When she opened her eyes again later, she was the only one left in the trailer.

She could smell bacon cooking, so she got up and pulled on her track pants and the same sweatshirt she wore the day before. Her father had moved the picnic table under the tarp and was cooking on the propane stove. Rain was still falling and puddles with floating pine needles surrounded the site. A yellow flip flop floated next to the pine tree.

Rica heard voices and saw her mother and sisters coming down the road, huddled under the blue and red golf umbrella that they always kept in the trailer for rainy days.

"Good morning!" her mother called cheerily. "Ooh, bacon and pancakes! It's a feast! Set the table for breakfast, please, girls."

"What a crappy morning!" Michelle complained. "What are we going to do all day?"

"We can go into town. We could use some groceries anyway," their mother suggested.

"Whoo-hoo! A trip into the big city of Northbrook," Michelle answered sarcastically.

"You don't need to come if it's not exciting enough for you, Shelley," her mother replied with an edge in her voice. Michelle hated being called Shelley. It had been a childhood nickname, and she had asked them ages ago to stop using it.

"It'll be especially boring for *you* to go into town again, won't it, Rica?" Michelle asked pointedly. Rica's head shot up and she felt her neck flush. She saw Michelle's chin rise defiantly.

"What do you mean, 'again'?" her father asked as he served the bacon.

Michelle's mouth twisted slightly and she

turned away to get the cutlery. "Oh, nothing," she answered. "We've all just been into Northbrook so many times. Every year." Rica felt herself breathe a sigh of relief.

After breakfast, Petra announced that she was going to stay in the trailer and read.

"I'm going to stay too," Michelle said casually. "I want to go for a run. You might pass me on your way home."

"I'll stay here as well," Rica decided.

"No, you have to come with us," her mother said firmly. "I think you should get your hair cut. It's been like a bush with this humidity."

"Oh, lucky you, Rica," Michelle commented as she walked over to the sheltered table. "A Northbrook haircut. I bet they have some great stylists there."

"Don't be too critical, or I'll take you in for a cut as well," her mother threatened.

Rica knew that arguing would have been pointless. As she climbed into the car after breakfast, she looked back and saw Michelle sitting at the table under the tarp, her yellow rain jacket setting a startling contrast to the dreary campground. The rain had almost stopped, but the wind was high and drops fell in mini-showers from the overhanging trees. Her father honked the horn as the car headed away from the site, but Michelle didn't look up.

* * *

After Rica's haircut – which she had to admit was a vast improvement – her father pulled into the General Store.

"Aren't you coming in with us?" Rica's mother asked as she and Rica's father got out of the car.

"I'll just stay here and take a little nap," she told them, yawning dramatically. She looked through the storefront window and saw the old-timer staring at her. She let her hair fall forward, cursing the fresh cut, and tipped her seat back until she was out of his view.

Fifteen minutes later, Rica's parents exited the store, placed a few grocery bags in the back seat, and they all headed back to the lake. By the time they had finished in town, more than two hours had passed. The rain had stopped, and the sun was making a valiant effort to break through the clouds. They pulled into the campsite and stepped carefully out of the van, avoiding the remains of scattered puddles that had yet to be absorbed by the soil.

"Hey, Michelle!" Rica called as they unloaded the van. "We've got groceries that need to be put away. Do you think you could help?"

"She's not here," Petra answered from inside the tent. "She's gone for a run."

"By herself?" Rica asked suspiciously.

"How would I know? She doesn't report to me."

"Thanks for your help," Rica muttered.

It only took a few minutes to place the groceries into the storage boxes they kept for food supplies. Rica then played a few games of Boggle with her parents until the sun had won its battle with the clouds.

"We could head to the beach now if you want," her mother said. Rica kept looking up the road as if she was expecting someone.

"Sure. I'll just change quickly," Rica said. She went into the trailer and started to put her swimsuit on.

"Coming, Petra?" her mother called from outside.

"No. I want to finish this book."

Rica was stepping down from the trailer when Craig and Finney ambled over and said they'd go to the beach too. She was pleased to have the extra company, even if it was just her cousin and his friend, and the three of them followed her parents down to the sand.

Rica and the boys sat down on a picnic table on the grassy ridge above the beach and talked as they watched more people wander down from the parking lot. As the sun got warmer, Rica finally took off her sweatshirt and lay back across the bench with her arm across her eyes. She didn't look over, but she could feel Finney's eyes on her again. He was getting annoying. Finney had known her since she was ten, and now, all of sudden, he was looking at her as if she was someone he had just met. It was weird.

"Hey, is that Michelle down there with that guy we played baseball with yesterday?" Craig asked.

Rica bolted upright and squinted to peer down the beach. It was Michelle, all right. She was wearing a bikini top with her shorts, swaying back and forth and swinging her hair in what Rica described as 'that annoying way she has.' Every now and again she would run her hand back from her forehead to sweep the hair away, but it always fell right back across her eyes again. Some people found that attractive. Rica found it irritating.

Her heart fell as she realized that Craig had been right. Michelle was talking to Stefan. She recognized his casual stance, his tousled hair, his toned arms. She watched them for a moment longer until they turned and walked up the embankment at the end of the beach and through the trees until they were out of sight.

Finney was looking at her with a knowing smirk. "Uh-oh," he said. "You got the hots for that guy?" It was said as if he didn't care, as though it was meant to be funny.

"Get real," Rica said, climbing off the bench. "He's not even my type."

"Your type? Since when do you have a type?" Craig laughed. "You've never even had a boyfriend, have you?"

"Too funny," Rica said dryly. She pulled her sweatshirt back on and tried to look indifferent. "Tell my Mom and Dad I went for a walk."

Craig chortled as she walked away haughtily. She slowed down when she was out of their sight. She wondered what she should do. Try to find Michelle and Stefan and act surprised to see them together? Go back to the campsite and hope they would wander back there? She opted for taking a walk, and if they happened to cross her path, well, she'd figure out what to do then.

She walked for almost an hour and a half, circling each campground, stopping for a few minutes on the north beach and then winding her way back toward the site. When she got to the ball diamond, she saw Kyle, Stefan, and Michelle walking across the grass toward the playground.

"Hey!" Stefan called across the park. "Rica! What're you doing here?"

She tried to look surprised to see them. "Hi!" she called, turning and walking toward them. Michelle looked annoyed to see her. Rica smiled broadly.

"I'm just out for a walk. Sometimes I just need to get away from the family, you know?"

"Since when?" Michelle asked. "You're the biggest Daddy's Girl ever!"

Rica ignored her and smiled even more brightly at Stefan. "I was down at the beach with Craig and Finney, but it got pretty cool down there, so I decided to go for a walk to warm up. I just love to go for walks, don't you?"

Michelle was looking at Rica as if she was from Mars. Rica ran her hand through her newly-trimmed hair the way she had seen Michelle do a thousand times. She tried to sway her hips, but she couldn't get a rhythm going so she stopped.

"We were just heading to your campsite," Kyle said. "Michelle was getting cold and wanted to get a sweater."

"Oh, that's good. Maybe we could all play a game of Boggle," Rica said, before seeing Michelle's face shrink back in apparent horror. She could only assume that playing games was something only a nerd would suggest. "Or not. We don't have to play. I mean ..." she scrambled for another idea, "we could just hang out here or at the beach ..."

"Sure, Boggle is good," Kyle said. Michelle glared at Rica. Kyle continued, "I used to play that a lot. I'm pretty good at it." He smiled at her.

"Okay, cool. We have some other games too. Balderdash, Pictionary ..." She looked at Michelle's face. Obviously for Michelle, her suggestions were getting worse and worse. "Or maybe Backgammon."

"Pictionary! I love that game," Stefan declared. Rica smiled at him encouragingly and took perverse pleasure in seeing Michelle scowl behind his shoulder.

"I love games too," Michelle said, stepping up beside the boys and making an effort to smile as brightly as she could. "We're just a game loving family, aren't we *baby* sister?"

Rica ignored the jibe and nodded. "It's true. We spend every minute we can together, playing games, sharing fun times ..." she put her arm around Michelle's shoulders, "just being pals, right *Shelly*?"

Michelle pulled away from Rica and fell behind, crossing her arms across her chest in anger. They went the rest of the way to the campsite in silence and arrived there at the same time as her parents came up from the water.

"Hi boys!" her mother called out. "Joining us for supper? We're just having hamburgers tonight but we've got lots."

"Sure," Stefan said. Kyle added his agreement. "We're really here for the Boggle championship though. Or, if I lose that, the Pictionary championship," Kyle said.

"Oh no!" Rica's father laughed. "No one beats me at Pictionary, boys. I am the Rembrandt of my time!" Michelle turned toward Rica and rolled her eyes.

Petra slammed her book shut. "What is this, a party or something?"

"We're going to play games," Rica

announced.

"Oh. Games." She headed for the tent. "I'll watch, I guess. Just let me get something warmer on."

"Grab me a sweater too," Michelle called to Petra. She yawned and stretched her arms outward, a move that Rica knew was made to deliberately accentuate her figure. Rica saw Stefan and Kyle look at each other with a smile. She was embarrassed for Michelle. Why did she do things like that?

By ten o'clock that night, the fire was blazing, bowls of popcorn were being devoured, and they were all enjoying a raucous competition of Pictionary.

Rica sat next to Stefan on the bench of the picnic table, and Michelle settled in on his other side. He seemed quite content to joke with both girls. Rica couldn't tell whether he had put his arm around her once or whether he was just trying to get some leverage to get up from the table. Michelle kept laughing and leaning against him, and at one point, Rica thought she saw Stefan put his hand on her knee under the table. Kyle was sitting across from them and seemed to be watching them all with amused interest. In fact, Rica noticed, Kyle and Stefan frequently seemed to be exchanging amused glances.

Finney sat in a lawn chair at the end of the picnic table and played with the same determination to win that he displayed in sports. When he and Alan clocked in fastest on "The Iceman Cometh," Finney slammed his pencil down and raised his arms in a sign of victory. Rica saw him trying to catch her eye. She ignored him, picked up her pencil, and prepared to draw 'The Sound of Music.'"

At about 11:45, her father stretched and stood up. "That's about it, guys. It's getting too late for us to be this noisy. Someone will report us to the rangers." He was right. They *had* been noisy.

They said good night to Stefan and Kyle who then headed down the road with a borrowed flashlight. Rica wistfully watched them leave, and then saw Michelle glaring at her again. Glaring was getting to be a habit of hers.

"What?" Rica demanded, before getting her toothbrush and towel from the trailer for the nightly trek to the main washrooms. "You keep giving me dirty looks!"

Michelle reached into her tent and found her toothbrush before zipping the tent closed. Her father winced and turned from folding the lawn chairs to tell the girls in hushed tones to keep the noise down.

"Sorry. We're just heading to the washroom," Michelle told her parents in an exaggerated whisper. "Are you coming, Petra?"

"Yeah," Petra replied, and then poured the last of her hot chocolate onto the fire, picked up a flashlight, and walked over to join her sisters. "You guys aren't going to fight all the way there though, are you?"

They walked away from the light of the campsite and allowed their eyes to adjust to the darkness of the gravel road. Petra turned on the flashlight and walked a few steps in front of the other two girls. "What's up with you two, anyway? I could tell there was something wrong all night."

Michelle snorted. "If Rica would stop drooling all over my boyfriend, there wouldn't be a problem."

"*Your* boyfriend? You mean Stefan?" Rica laughed hollowly.

"Yes, Stefan. We hung out together today and he said he really likes me."

"In your dreams," Rica said. "He told me that he likes *me*! We were kissing for practically an hour yesterday!" She gave Michelle a look that said to try and top that one.

Michelle's steps slowed and she turned an anxious face toward her sister. "Oh, Rica. You're kidding, right?"

Rica stopped walking. "No. Why would I kid about it? He likes *me*."

"I knew you had a crush on him, but I didn't think he'd actually *do* anything with you. I mean, you're too young for him." Michelle's face was solemn. "Stefan told me he could get serious about someone like me, and I believe him. I was making out with him today, and I don't mean just kissing. You can ask Kyle. He came into the tent this afternoon and saw us." Rica could see that her sister wasn't lying.

"What do you mean, not just kissing?" Rica demanded. She was furious that Michelle would have gone to such lengths to get Stefan to pay attention to her. It was obvious that she was just jealous of the interest that Stefan had shown in Rica. But then she thought back to the way he had been behaving at their campsite – the way he had touched Michelle, the looks he had exchanged with Kyle – and she realized that he really may have been playing the girls for fools. She felt her eyes begin to fill with tears and turned away so that Michelle wouldn't see.

Petra turned and pointed the flashlight at her sisters.

"Don't you two know anything?" Petra asked them, shaking her head in disbelief. "Every year it happens. People like us come up to the park, get bored with the beach, start looking to see if there's anyone interesting around, and the next thing you know – summer fling. And because everyone goes home in a week or two, there's no commitment, so a guy like Stefan can fool around with the two of you and never have to pay the price, you know what I mean?"

She turned and started walking again, and her sisters were forced to follow in order to stay within reach of the flashlight beam.

"I think he really likes me though," Rica said unconvincingly, as though to herself.

"Yeah. That's why he was with me today. To get to you." Michelle's voice was bitter. "He couldn't care less about you, Rica."

"Or you." Rica kicked a large stone on the gravel road. She wished it was Michelle's head.

The girls were quiet until they could see the lights of the central washrooms shining ahead of them.

"What did you mean by 'pay the price'?"

Michelle suddenly asked Petra. "You said that guys like him never have to pay the price."

The older sister shrugged. "You know, get the same back. Get dumped or something."

Michelle suddenly grabbed Rica's arm and swung her around so that they were facing each other.

"We have to get back at him," Michelle said, her eyes gleaming, her lips curled into a wry smile. "He's going home soon, and he'll be telling all his friends about what a great summer he had messing with half the girls he met on vacation. I don't know about you, but I'm not going to let him make a fool out of me!"

Rica looked at her doubtfully. "I'm mad too. But I don't see what we can do about it, aside from telling him what a creep he is," she added.

Petra turned off the flashlight and stood with her hand on her hip, waiting. "Come on, you guys. Are we going into the washroom or what?" She turned and started walking across the grass toward the brick building.

"Wait! Petra, you need to help us." Michelle ran up and grabbed Petra, blocking her way to the washrooms. "You're our bait! We can use you to play a trick on Stefan! We need to try to stick together, right?" She reached for Rica's hand and squeezed it excitedly. Rica had to smile slightly at the idea of joining forces with her sisters.

Petra sighed and looked up at the sky. Rica wondered if she was considering that this was probably the last summer that the three of them would ever spend on vacation together. Petra would be working next summer to earn money for college. Rica looked at her eagerly, her eyebrows raised in anticipation.

"I can't believe I'm considering this. What do you have in mind?" Petra asked Michelle with resignation.

Michelle jumped up and down, hugging Petra with unbridled excitement. "I have no idea," she admitted. "I just know it'll take the three of us to make it work."

"I won't even ask what that's about," their father said dryly as he and their mother walked past the girls on their way up the hill to the floodlit washrooms. The girls didn't talk any more until their parents were well out of hearing range.

"Let me think it over tonight," Petra told the girls, grinning as they stood before her eagerly. "Believe me, I'll come up with something that Stefan will never forget."

Chapter 7

Rica had a restless night. She kept replaying every contact that she'd had with Stefan, trying to remember everything he had said, how he had looked at her, whether or not he had seemed really serious about liking her when he had been kissing her so eagerly. *How could he have faked that?* she wondered. And why did Michelle make out with him when she knew that Rica had gone off alone with him the night before? Did she really believe that he was just a friend, or did she care so little for her sister's feelings that she would stomp all over them this way?

By the time she fell asleep, Rica had lost track of just who the enemy was – the boy who was playing games with her, or the sister who wanted him for herself. Either way, it hurt enough to make her wish she had never gotten involved with him. Her only hope of redeeming this vacation now rested in whatever revenge plan Petra was plotting. She'd have to worry about Michelle later.

"What would you like to do today?" Rica's father asked as Rica came out of the trailer the next morning. "Canoeing? Cycling?"

She poured herself a glass of juice and sat down on the bench of the picnic table.

"No thanks, Dad. Michelle and Petra and I are going to hang out together around here for the day."

"Really?" Her father looked surprised. "Together?" He was probably thinking that it wasn't often that the three girls did anything together willingly.

"It's just you and me then, Honey," he said as Rica's mother came over to the site carrying a bucket of water. "The girls are busy on their own today. Let's see if Alan and Joanne feel like biking."

Petra and Michelle came out of their tent, giggling together. Rica saw her parents look at each other in amazement.

"I could get used to this," her father said, nodding toward the two girls who were in better spirits than usual.

"It'll never last," Rica heard her mother predict. "Come on. Let's head out before the bubble bursts." They unchained their bikes from the tree next to the tent and went off to convince Alan and Joanne to join them on their ride.

"Have fun!" Rica called after them, watching them round the corner at the end of their road. She turned back to her sisters and saw that they were already settled across from each other on the picnic table. She walked over to join them, careful to be seated on Petra's side of the table.

"Okay, so here's the plan," Petra said, turning toward Rica and gesturing excitedly. "We're going to invite the boys to a little party tonight ..."

"Not here," Michelle cut in. "Mom and Dad will be here, and ..."

"Up in the wilderness area on the far side of the park," Petra went on, ignoring her sister. "We'll meet them up there and spend some time around the fire, get them all relaxed, and when the time is right, I'll put the moves on Stefan. I'll lead him down to Canoe Lake and he'll think we're alone. Both of you watch us leave and then follow a few minutes after us. I'll convince him to go skinny-dipping with me. When he gets all his clothes off, you two will sneak out of the woods and take off with them. Then I'll catch up with you and we'll leave him there naked!"

Petra slapped her hands on the top of the picnic table and sat back with what Rica could only describe as a satisfied grin.

"Yes!" Michelle laughed. "That will be perfect payback! We'll grab all his clothes and throw them up into the trees, or take them back over to the campfire and burn them!" Her eyes were glowing with apparent excitement. She and Petra high-fived.

Rica looked skeptical. "Didn't we see that in a movie once? He'd have to be sort of stupid to fall for that, wouldn't he?"

Petra and Michelle looked at her as if she was to be pitied.

"Rica," Petra said as though she was talking to a five-year-old, "you don't have a lot of experience with boys. Believe me, he'll take off his clothes if I want him to."

"Where's your sense of drama?" Michelle stood up and came around the table to stand beside Petra. "Can't you just see him, standing naked in the woods and having to go back over to his campsite without any clothes on?"

Petra started to laugh, and it was infectious. "Oh, and you and Michelle have to make sure he knows it was you two who stole his clothes." She laughed again, and Rica started to laugh uncertainly with her.

"I like it," Michelle said. "It'll be hysterical. Come on, Rica. Don't be a prude."

Rica shrugged and nodded. "All right. It's pretty lame, but I guess I'm in."

"Come on then," Petra said, starting toward the road. "Let's go and extend a party invitation."

They headed up the road together in the direction of Kyle and Stefan's site. Rica listened to Michelle eagerly playing through scenarios of how the plan would work, and she began to see that Michelle was sincere in her desire to get back at Stefan. Like Rica, Michelle must have truly been hurt by his motives and actions. For the first time, she felt as though she and Michelle were sharing something together and that Petra was standing by them. It almost felt as if they were equals.

Rica couldn't remember the last time that

the three of them had done anything together that wasn't at the insistence of her parents. She walked taller, feeling as if she was finally part of their lives, the lives of her older sisters who had always seemed to have so much more freedom and more fun than she did. *Maybe my wish for an unforgettable vacation is still going to come true,* she thought with satisfaction.

"We're like Charlie's Angels," Rica said, thinking out loud.

Michelle chortled. "Sure, Short-Stuff. You be Drew Barrymore."

"I *love* Drew Barrymore," she said agreeably.

They approached site 412 and looked at the empty space in front of the tent.

"Hello?" Petra called out tentatively. "Stefan? Kyle?"

"Their car isn't here." Michelle indicated the spot where the black Sunfire should have been parked. "They must have gone into town."

"We can come back later," Rica said, but no sooner had she spoken than they heard a car approaching. They turned to see Kyle's old car rumbling toward the site. They all stepped back to allow room for the vehicle to turn in and park.

"Hey!" said Stefan, climbing out of the passenger seat and smiling at the girls. "Good timing on our part! We didn't know you were all coming."

"We just wanted to invite you to a little party," Petra said, looking coyly at Stefan as he leaned back against the car.

"Oh yeah? A party?" He grinned. "Then it's a good thing we bought that beer when we were in town with you. Right, Rica?"

Petra looked across at Rica with surprise. "Rica! I must have underestimated you." Rica suddenly felt a little proud of herself. She tilted her chin upward and let her hair fall across her shoulders.

"So where's the party?" Stefan asked.

"In the wilderness part of the park," Petra answered. "It's across the highway and about a ten-minute drive through the forest."

The boys both shook their heads and waited for her to continue.

"You'll love it. No one camps up there anymore. Lots of privacy," she added, looking up at Stefan flirtatiously from beneath her carefully curled lashes.

Stefan smiled slowly. Rica could almost

see him thinking that Petra was the best looking of the three sisters. It hurt a little, but if he fell for Petra, then the plan would work. *Stop caring,* she told herself. *Stop wanting him so much.*

"We can drive up together," Petra was saying. "I'll get the van from Dad and we'll pick you guys up here at 7:30. Sound good?"

"Sure. No problem," Kyle answered. The boys looked pleased with themselves, as if they had found a winning scratch ticket.

"See you later," Petra said in a promising voice. The three girls turned and walked away. Rica was conscious of the impression they were making from behind. She saw Michelle run her hand through her hair for good measure.

When they got far enough away, Michelle and Petra doubled over with laughter.

"Did you see him?" Michelle shrieked. "He was eating out of your hand! I thought he was going to grab you right there by the car!"

Rica watched the girls laughing. *How funny is that, really?* She hated to admit it to herself, but a part of her still liked Stefan, even after finding out that he had been fooling around with Michelle. The idea that he would be so entranced by her other sister wasn't all that great. In fact, she realized, she felt insulted.

Angry even.

Michelle looked over at Rica and straightened up, catching her breath. She studied her younger sister's face for a moment and then put her hand on her arm. "You know what they say, Rica. Don't get mad – get even."

Rica nodded, and started to walk. He had been flirting with Petra, right there in front of Michelle and her. How did he think he could get away with that? Just how many girls had he been with while he was here? *They're probably right – he deserves whatever he might get.*

She fell behind the others and let them chat together on the way back. Then she started to worry – what if Petra decided that she actually liked Stefan? It was entirely possible – he was hard to resist, even after his two-timing behavior had been discovered. Rica thought of the way Petra had spoken to him, the way she had looked at him. She shook her head and tried to erase the thought. They had to make this plan work. She took a deep breath, pushed aside her doubts, and tried to tell herself that nothing could possibly go wrong.

Chapter 8

After supper that night, Petra put on the tank top she had bought at a Madonna concert, a clean pair of low-riding jeans, and her boots with two-inch heels.

"What made you bring those camping?" Rica asked her, looking at the totally impractical boots and remembering her father's instructions to pack light.

"You just never know," Petra advised, "when you'll need to look good." Petra's nails were perfect and her hair was brushed to a golden sheen. It really didn't matter what she had on – she would have looked good in torn track pants and canvas sneakers.

"Don't forget to bring a sweater," she told

her sisters. "It'll be cool later." She pulled a light sweater out of her duffle bag in the tent and tied it loosely around her slim hips.

Michelle and Rica hadn't brought a variety of clothes to meet every occasion. They both dressed in their sandals, jeans, and sweatshirts, just as they had every day since arriving at the park. They had taken the 'pack light' instruction seriously. Rica waited until Michelle wasn't looking and then applied some of Petra's lipstick and mascara. *I might as well look good so he knows what he's losing*, she thought.

"Where are you kids heading?" their mother asked brightly as the girls emerged from the tent. Rica's parents had been cycling most of the day and were now sitting on the lawn chairs with their feet on the bench of the picnic table.

"Just meeting some friends," Petra replied.

"Well, behave yourselves," their father said. "And don't be too late coming back. And Rica, try to be quiet when you come into the trailer. I have a feeling your mother and I will be heading to bed early after all of our exercise today," her father said.

"I'm just going to grab a few snacks to take with us," Michelle called as she exchanged a look with Petra. Petra nodded, and Michelle went into the storage bin beside the trailer, grabbed a few things from the food box, slipped them into the back of the van, and winked at Petra.

"All set?" Petra asked her, glancing into the rear before slamming the back door of the van.

Michelle nodded and the three girls climbed into the vehicle. Petra had just started the engine when Rica heard Finney call out "Hey! Wait for us!" and she turned to see Craig and Finney cutting through the trees between the two campsites.

"We ran into Kyle this afternoon and he told us we could come with you," Craig said as he and his friend clambered into the van uninvited, Craig squeezing into the seat next to Rica, and Finney sliding the door closed before stretching out on the bench seat behind them.

"Where are Kyle and Stefan supposed to sit?" Michelle demanded, scowling at the boys from the front seat.

"They'll fit in somewhere," Craig assured her.

Michelle shook her head, and Rica knew that she was rolling her eyes as she turned back to the front. Petra waved good-bye to her parents, who were watching from their chairs, and pulled slowly out of the site. When she was out of view, she sped up and maneuvered the van along the narrow camp roads until she reached the boys' site.

"It'll be a little crowded in here," Petra apologized to Stefan as he climbed in and settled on the floor.

"No problem," he said, flashing a smile in her direction.

Kyle opened the rear door. "Gimme a second," he said, and he carried a heavy cooler from the picnic table and loaded it into the back, then walked over to his car, opened the trunk and took out a case of beer and transferred it to the van. "I've got a case on ice," he said, seeming pleased with himself. "I can sit back here with it." He climbed in the back of the van and closed the door behind himself before finding a spot on the floor.

"We're on our way then," Petra announced as she pulled away from the site. She drove away from the campground, through the park gates, and toward the wilderness park.

The sun was getting lower and there was already a chill in the air.

* * *

After driving five miles up the rugged logging road, Petra circled the old campgrounds more than once, finally stopping at a large clearing with vegetation creeping in from the surrounding forest. They would be well hidden from view, Rica realized, but it didn't matter – there was no one within miles. The wilderness sites had been closed for years.

"Maybe we should have brought firewood," Kyle suggested, pointing at the remnants of a fire pit in the center of the clearing.

"I'd say it's taken care of," Finney said, gesturing toward the endless trees.

When they were all out of the van, Rica busied herself gathering fallen twigs and branches, breaking them up into the circle of rocks that had once served as a fire pit. She was grateful for the distraction – she had become nervous after seeing Stefan carry the loaded cooler from the van.

When the fire was finally crackling, they settled onto logs and opened the cooler, a signal that the party was officially underway.

Some time later, Kyle pulled out a bottle from the melting ice, the cool water dripping down the wrinkled label and over his fingers. "Who wants another beer?" he asked. "Petra?"

"I'm not drinking," she said, holding up a bottle of water. She had whispered to Rica earlier that she had wanted to stay sober all night not only so that she could drive them all back to the site, but also so that she could think clearly when it came to executing the Stefan conspiracy. "I'm the designated driver," Petra reminded him.

Kyle snorted his disapproval and turned to the others. "Rica?"

Rica shook her head and noticed that it felt as if it moved in slow motion. She hadn't wanted to try a beer in the first place, but Stefan had kept offering and Michelle had been looking at her with a smirk, so Rica had finally taken the bottle. The first sip had been pretty gross. She must have made a face because Michelle had laughed at her. That had given her the encouragement to try again, but the beer tasted just as bad on the second swig as it had on the first. She had never liked the smell of beer and it tasted exactly how she had expected it to taste – like old socks. *Why do people drink this stuff?* she had wondered as she sat studying the label. *Five percent alcohol. That doesn't seem like much,* she thought. *Ninety-five percent water.*

She was on her fourth one now and it was only about nine thirty.

Everyone was seated around the campfire. Each of them was balanced on folded blankets placed on a couple of logs that had been rolled to either side of the fire pit. There was an old picnic table on the site, and they had moved it between the two logs so that seating was arranged in a triangle around the circle of rocks that contained the fire. Craig and Finney had come over to sit on the log next to Rica, who was sitting with her knees hugged close to her chest. The fire cast a warm glow of moving color across the faces of Michelle and Kyle who were on the bench across from them, while Stefan sat a few feet away on the other log.

A few minutes later, Michelle stood up and went to the rear of the van.

"Anyone up for some of this?" she asked, walking back from the van holding a bottle of vodka and smiling mischievously at the group.

"Hey! Where did you get that?" Stefan asked, his eyes sparkling as he rose and walked over to take the bottle from her.

"It was hidden in the van. We brought it

from our campsite," Michelle said proudly.

Rica felt the hair on the back of her neck rise.

"You mean it's Mom and Dad's? You *stole* it?" She shook her head in disbelief, remembering the look her sisters had exchanged at the site earlier that evening. "You guys are in so much trouble! Dad's going to know it was you. He's going to kill you!"

"We couldn't come empty handed," Petra explained patiently, as if she was talking to an idiot. "Not when the boys are nice enough to share their beer with us."

"Stop being such a baby," Michelle laughed. "Honestly Rica, if you can't just have fun with us, then you shouldn't have come. Maybe you should just go back to the site and go to bed."

Stefan was watching with amusement. Rica felt her face flush with embarrassment and anger. So much for feeling as though she and her sisters were equals. Why would they humiliate her now in front of everyone?

"I'm not leaving," Rica asserted. "But Dad's going to be looking for that, in fact he's probably already noticed it's missing, and I'm not going to be the one to take the blame for it when he asks where it went."

"Like anyone ever blames you for anything," Michelle pointed out.

"Are we going to talk about it all night, or are we going to drink it?" Finney asked, taking the bottle from Stefan and twisting the cap off. "Who has a glass?"

"You don't need a glass," Petra answered. "Do it like it's a shooter. Just take a quick swig."

Finney raised the bottle to his mouth and tipped it up, swallowing several times.

"Just a bit at a time!" Petra said sharply. "You'll make yourself sick if you drink too fast."

"Here," Craig said, taking the bottle from his friend.

Craig tipped the bottle and swallowed the liquid, then leaned forward and started to cough. Stefan grabbed the bottle from his hand to stop it from spilling. Craig continued to choke.

"Jeez, buddy, you could have dropped the bottle. Or worse yet, hacked up into it!" Stefan yelled. He then stepped toward Rica and held the vodka out to her. "Do you want a slug?"

She saw the bottle poised before her, saw

Stefan's questioning face, Michelle's cynical smirk, Finney's daring eyes. She saw herself reach for the bottle, heard herself answer "Sure."

The bottle felt heavy in her hand. The liquid was clear, like water. She studied the label. *Forty percent alcohol. Triple distilled for exceptional purity*. She raised it to her nose. It was nothing like the overpowering smell of the beer she had been drinking, and she had gotten used to that. This had barely any scent at all. *This might not be so bad*, she thought.

She put the bottle to her lips and closed her eyes. She could hear Michelle laughing, telling everyone that Rica was too much of a baby to ever really do it, that she would just touch the bottle to her lips and pretend to drink, that she would say she had done it, but that she wouldn't have the guts to take a good swig. She opened her eyes again and looked across the bottle at Stefan's face. He was waiting to see if Michelle was right, a small smile playing at the edges of his lips. Rica tipped the bottle and swallowed, and then swallowed again.

A cheer rose from all of the others. She gave them all a triumphant grin and passed the vodka back to Stefan. He winked at her as he moved back to sit on the log next to Petra.

"You going to pass that around or what?" Craig asked, watching as Stefan took several swigs.

"Sorry man," Stefan said, passing the bottle.

"Just leave enough in the bottle so I can take it back, fill it with some water, and leave it where I found it," Michelle warned.

Rica wondered if Michelle really thought they could polish off most of a bottle of liquor and have it go unnoticed by their parents. Then the thought passed as she was suddenly overcome by the warmth that was spreading through her chest, and when the bottle came back around to her, she did not hesitate to tip it back and have another gulp. And then another.

Craig rose unevenly from his end of the log, swayed slightly, and then leaned over to grab another piece of wood for the blaze. Despite well-fed flames that were already shooting up about four feet, he tossed a large piece into the center, causing sparks to play through the air like fireflies.

Finney's foot had been resting on a rock next to the campfire. The sole of his shoe was starting to smoke and he didn't even seem to notice. Rica watched the smoke rise, took another drink from the long-necked beer bottle, and began to giggle

She turned and watched as Michelle did what she always did best – entertain. No matter what she thought of Michelle, Rica had to admit that no one could tell a story the way Michelle could, dragging it out with actions and reactions so that it was almost a ten-minute long, one-woman show. Rica laughed along with the others, at one point having to wipe tears from her eyes. She had never liked the way Michelle monopolized attention, but having had a few drinks, she could see why everyone liked being around her so much.

Rica was surprised to find Stefan watching her. She smiled with more confidence than usual and twisted her hair absently around her finger. He smiled back and locked his eyes on hers. But then Petra walked behind him and ran her hand across the back of his shoulders as she passed. He turned his head and watched her as she leaned over to add some wood to the fire. Rica felt a pang of jealousy.

Michelle was trying to get everyone to sing camp songs that they had learned when they were kids. No one else seemed to be joining in except Rica, who was soon singing along to a ridiculous round of 'Swimming,

swimming, in the swimming pool' and ignoring the looks that others exchanged when she started into the third verse. Michelle lost interest and started talking to Kyle, so Rica carried on alone. There were actions to do with the song and Rica did them with vigor, exaggerating the breaststroke and diving motions with each stanza.

"Have another drink," Kyle snorted, and she stopped singing and took a long swig. *Good stuff,* she thought lazily. Her body was tingling all over and when she touched her hand to her face, it was as if her hand was someone else's.

When she looked around the fire again, Petra and Stefan were gone.

"Michelle," Rica said, turning to the bench of the picnic table where Michelle sat talking to Kyle, her face soft in the flickering glow of the campfire, her eyes glued to Kyle's face as if she'd never seen him before. She was talking more quietly than was normal for Michelle, and her hand kept reaching across to touch his arm.

"Michelle!" Rica repeated.

Michelle looked over at her, and her eyes hardened slightly.

"What?" *Butt out,* her expression seemed

to be saying.

"Petra's gone. And Stefan." Rica wanted to stand up, but she wasn't sure her legs could support her. Her knees felt funny, as if the booze had settled there and would make a sloshy sound if she tried to walk.

"That's okay. Leave her alone," Michelle said. She went back to talking to Kyle.

Rica scratched her neck and looked back around the fire. Craig was sitting on the other end of the log, staring at the fire as though he was mesmerized. His face looked ghoulish, his eyes glazed. *He's had way too much to drink*, she thought. No sooner had the thought passed through her mind than he turned slightly and leaned over, throwing up behind the log.

"Gross!" Michelle said, turning to look at her cousin. "You are *so* disgusting!"

Craig wiped his mouth on his sleeve and sat upright again, swaying only slightly. He continued to stare absently at the fire.

"Man, you guys are really wasted!" Kyle said, looking at Craig and then across at Rica. *Me? Why is he looking at me?* she thought to herself.

A moment later, the bottle she was holding slipped through her fingers. It dropped to the ground beside her foot and rolled slightly until it caught on a clump of weeds between her shoe and the leg of the picnic table beside her. A trickle of liquid ran from the neck of the bottle and drained toward the fire, leaving a narrow trench in its wake. Rica stared at it for what could have been seconds, minutes, hours.

A piercing shriek brought her back to the moment. Kyle was tickling Michelle and she had fallen from the bench, laughing.

"The *plan,*" Rica announced suddenly. "We have to find Petra and Stefan. They've gone swimming," Rica added, in case anyone was listening.

"Who's gone swimming?" Finney asked as he stumbled toward her and planted himself on the log next to her.

"My sister. And Stefan. We have to find them. It's a plan." She spoke deliberately and with great intensity.

"All right then. I'll go with you," he agreed.

"But Michelle is supposed to come." Rica leaned closer to him. "*Michelle.*"

"Yeah, okay, but I think she's kind of busy." He nodded toward the picnic table. Michelle was back sitting next to Kyle, her head on his shoulder, eyes closed.

"Can't I go with you to find them?" he asked her. Rica looked at him and thought how soft his face looked. Everything looked soft. The flames of the fire, the trees, the log.

"Yeah. You can be Michelle. I'll call you Shelley." She giggled. "Come on Shelley. Follow me. We have to go to the lake."

"The beach?" he asked. "We'd need the van to ..."

"No! Not the beach," she hissed. "The *lake*. Canoe Lake. It's down the road and through the woods. And they'll be there *in the nude*. We gotta go do the *plan*."

She stood up and swayed until he caught her arm.

"I'll bring a blanket in case we get cold," he said, taking the one from beneath them on the log and tossing it over his arm. "Are you okay to walk if I hold your arm?"

"I'm perfect," she said with confidence. "I'm better than I've ever been. I'm a walking machine!"

He took her arm and started down the sandy trail away from the fire. The temperature was cool as they moved farther from the flames.

"Canoe Lake," he said. "I've never even

heard of it ..."

"It's not far. Down the road and through the woods and down the hill and over the hill ..." Her voice was like a song. Her feet felt huge. She started to giggle. "Am I walking funny?" she asked him. "Are my feet big or what?" She took exaggerated steps, her knees rising higher than usual, her feet pointed outwards.

"You're hilarious, Rica," he said. She made note that even when she was wearing big feet, he seemed to think that she was okay. Maybe Finney was all right. Maybe Finney was kind of cute.

"Down here?" he asked, looking doubtfully at a trail that led off the road and down an embankment through the woods.

"Yes!" she hissed. "It's a surprise though, so we have to be *quiet*."

Finney nodded and moved in front of her. "It's going to have to be single file. I'll go in front of you, and you keep a hand on my shoulder so that you don't fall."

She saluted him and then put her hand onto his right shoulder. She started to sing in a falsetto that sounded nothing like her own voice. "Lean on me, when you're not stroong, and I'll be your friend, I'll help you carr-ry o-on ..."

"That's great," he assured her. "But aren't we supposed to be quiet or something?"

"Oh! *Shhhhh!*" she hissed. "We have to sneak up on them."

They walked in silence for several minutes.

"I hear voices," Finney whispered.

"It's *them*," Rica announced knowingly. "They're in the water."

The sound of splashing was audible, confirming what she had said. Petra could be heard giggling, and Stefan was calling her name, telling her to swim over to him.

"We have to find their clothes," Rica whispered. "We have to hide them."

"Why do you want to hide their clothes?" Finney had stopped walking and was standing next to a tree with Rica leaning against his back, peering around his shoulder.

"*His* clothes. Just his clothes." She started to laugh. "He has to be naked. That'll teach him."

Finney looked skeptical. "Yeah, that'll teach him all right. What are you trying to teach him?"

She swatted his arm. "That he can't fool around with me *and* my sisters. It's just not right."

"Oh." He switched the blanket he was carrying to his other arm so that he could steady her.

"Come on. We have to find his clothes." She pushed past Finney and started to pat the ground around the trees. The edge of the forest opened out onto the lake, and the moon provided enough light that they could see the water and the shadows of Petra and Stefan in the middle of the small bay.

"Here! Here they are," Rica said excitedly as she touched a pile of discarded clothing.

"Who is that?" Stefan called from the water. "Is someone there?"

Rica clamped her hand over her mouth and turned to Finney with wide eyes. She pointed at the clothes in a pile by their feet and they both bent to sort them, and then grabbed the jeans and sweater that Stefan had been wearing.

"The underwear, the underwear!" Rica said to Finney, and they tossed the clothes around in a desperate effort to retrieve the underwear before Stefan could swim over and see what was happening.

"There isn't any!" Finney whispered. "He

must be wearing it!"

"Oh, what a loser!" Rica announced in a loud whisper. "Petra said she could get anyone to take their clothes off ..."

"Who is that? Is that you, Kyle? Michelle?" Stefan's voice was closer. He must have been swimming toward shore.

"*Run!*" Rica squealed, and she turned and tripped over her feet, landing on the trail without ceremony. Finney helped her to her feet and they stumbled up the path, laughing and shouting as they pushed and pulled each other up the hill toward the road.

"We did it!" Rica shrieked as they left the woods and stepped onto the gravel of the road. "Michelle didn't help, but you did and you're just as good as Michelle any day. Maybe even better!" She flung her arms round Finney's neck, her hands still clutching socks and a rumpled sweater. Her face crushed into his chest and her hair brushed against his neck and chin.

Finney reached down and turned her face upward, and then his lips were on hers. She kissed him back and wondered if her breath was as bad as his was, all stale beer and greasy chips.

"Come on," he said, urging her forward.

"Let's get out of here in case they're following us."

He took her hand and pulled her along. The camp road forked in several directions and he turned without hesitation. Rica simply followed without question.

When they stopped, they were in the clearing of a campsite. Rica listened to hear if Petra and Stefan had followed, but there was no one, there was nothing.

"It's so quiet," she said simply.

"It's just us," Finney agreed. He tossed Stefan's jeans onto the ground and then spread the blanket carefully onto the pine needles that covered the site.

"Come on," he said, taking her hand. "Come and lie down with me."

Rica's head was spinning and she thought that lying down might be the best idea anyone had had all evening. She let herself be led forward, and she sank onto the blanket gratefully.

"It's kind of cold now," she said, feeling the chill of the damp ground through the fibers of the woolen blanket.

"I'll keep you warm," he offered, and he leaned his chest onto hers and kissed her tentatively and then again with conviction.

She kissed him back and wondered if he could be convinced to wear something other than red and yellow floral bathing trunks on the beach. He was a good kisser. He was kind of a nice guy. She thought maybe Stefan had been a bit of a loser anyway. For a second, she wondered if Finney would have been interested in her at all if he hadn't seen her interest in Stefan. Maybe it was all just a game for him. But he really was a good kisser.

The rough wool of the blanket felt scratchy under her back. Her sweatshirt had ridden up, or maybe he had pulled it up. She wasn't sure. Her head felt like cotton, all spun and wispy, without substance. The stars looked like pinpricks in the blackness of the sky, and she watched them swell and then retract as though connected to her heartbeat.

She hardly knew what was happening at first, but then she was aware that Finney was talking to her, saying something about how much he liked her. He was too close, his breath too hot on her face, and she wanted to move away, but the sky was closing down on them, holding them there.

"Finney ..." she protested weakly.

His hands were on her arms, pinning her to the ground, then they were moving, pressing against the outside of her sweatshirt, moving toward her breasts.

"Finney, you're hurting me ..."

He didn't seem to hear. His body fell beside her on the ground, and she felt his hands sliding under her sweater and then fumbling with her jeans.

"Finney – *stop*," she repeated. She felt herself starting to panic, her breath changing to shallow gasps. She willed herself to move, to push him away and to roll over and stagger to her feet. He called her name and reached up for her, but she was backing away, looking at him as though he was a stranger. She was suddenly terrified of Finney, of herself, of what was happening. She turned away from him and ran.

Chapter 9

It was impossibly, terrifyingly dark in the midst of the trees. The night sky had been clear and star filled, wondrous and romantic when Rica first lay on the ground next to Finney. But that had been in the open space of the wilderness campsite, and now she was hopelessly closed in by the threatening blackness of the endless woods.

His voice had followed her when she first ran into the forest, but she couldn't tell if he was coming after her. Still, she had stumbled into the woods, compelled to get as far away from him as she could. She was driven by her fear.

She had no sense of where she had been or where she was heading. The ground felt as if it might be sloping slightly downward, and it was getting softer beneath her sandals. She hoped that she would eventually either get back to the site where Michelle, Craig, and Kyle had stayed, or come out by the main road. Either way, she would be able to get home safely.

She continued to push her way through the trees, steadying herself by bracing her hands against each as she passed, stopping regularly to listen for voices and to watch for the glow of a campfire.

Her foot caught a large rock and she stumbled, the sudden jolt making her stomach turn. She held onto the trunk of the nearest tree and bent over to throw up. When she was finished, she realized how frightening the situation was and how helpless she felt. She sank to the ground and sobbed.

* * *

"She's been missing for over half an hour!" Petra said urgently. "Finney tried to find her first, then he came and found Stefan and me, and the three of us went looking for her. We were yelling and yelling – couldn't you hear us?" Her face was white in the beam of the flashlight that Kyle had pointed toward her.

"We didn't hear anything," Michelle said defensively. "We were here the whole time, but you must have been too far away. And our charming cousin Craig is completely done for the night," she said, waving her hand toward where he lay passed out on the ground.

"Well, come and help us," Petra urged. "She could be deep in the woods by now, and it's so dark ..."

"She'll have to come out onto a camp road at some point, won't she?" Michelle asked as she picked up a flashlight. "Don't all these roads turn in circles or something? I mean, how can someone get lost in a campground?" She sounded amazed by Rica's apparent stupidity.

"God, Michelle," Kyle said as he pulled his jacket on. "It's your sister. Don't you want to find her?"

"Of course I do," she huffed. "I just think it's typical that everything has to stop for Rica. She always has been the center of attention. She's probably just hiding somewhere to make us worry."

Petra shook her head and gave the second flashlight they had to Kyle. "That's horrible, Michelle. Wake Craig up and bring him with us. I want to get back there quickly and start looking again."

* * *

Rica decided to turn back and try to retrace her steps to the spot where she had left Finney. Running alone in the forest made no sense, and she was sure that Finney would have sobered up in the time she had been wandering. It didn't take her long, however, to realize that retracing steps through the dark was impossible.

Her sweatshirt was not nearly warm enough for the bone-chilling cold. She was sure that by now it must be the middle of the night. If so, she had been wandering for hours. The damp air felt as if it was cutting through her. It made her legs so stiff that walking was becoming difficult.

"Michelle!" she yelled as loudly as possible. "Petra!" She listened and then yelled again. There was no response.

The branches scratched her face and legs. The pain was sharper than before, a sign that meant she was almost sober. She listened again, straining, hoping to hear voices in the distance, praying that everyone was looking for her.

"Michelle! Petra!" Her voice pierced through the night.

Her foot slipped on a damp root as she edged her way between the trees. She felt herself losing balance, and her sandal suddenly caught on something. Her foot twisted and pulled loose from the shoe, causing her to stumble. Her bare foot fell and, as she tried to catch her balance, sank several inches into a patch of black and oozing mud. Instantly she was overcome by nightmarish visions of leaches and snakes, winding, clinging, drawing blood. Her foot jerked upward and she shrieked, unashamedly.

* * *

Petra held the small flashlight shakily and pointed it toward the ground so that she could see where to place her steps.

"I'm sorry I didn't take it seriously at first," Michelle said earnestly, grabbing Petra's arm and following her through the trees. "I'm really worried now. How long has it been? It feels like hours."

"I don't know. This is crazy. We've probably covered some of the same ground twice, but it's so hard to tell. Where are the boys?"

"Over on the left." She stopped and listened for a moment, then yelled "Craig!"

A faint response could be heard somewhere ahead of them.

"I can't even tell where they are, can you?" Michelle asked, inching behind Petra in the darkness. The small beam of the flashlight bounced eerily off the ground in front of them, but was not powerful enough to cut any distance through the trees.

Petra shook her head. "We're making a big mistake. We're going to end up losing someone else. Let's turn around."

"Turn around? What if she's just up ahead?" Michelle blocked the way and put her hands on Petra's arms. "What if she's hurt or something ...?"

"We have to." Petra pressed her sister to turn around. "I want to go back. We need to tell Mom and Dad."

* * *

The ground was soft, covered in layers of leaves from autumns past, now damp and pressed into a soft mass between the ancient roots. Rica lay down and curled into as small a space as possible, her arms and legs drawn tight to her chest for warmth. Her hand clutched the ruined sandal that she had pulled from the tangle of roots nearby. A leather strap had been torn loose from the shoe; it was utterly useless now.

Rica's nostrils filled with the deep, overpowering pungency of rotting soil. Isolation and the dark of night overwhelmed her. Her breath was short – she remembered the asthma attacks she used to have when she was younger and willed herself to calm down and take deep breaths.

There was a creaking in the trees. She didn't know what could be causing it as there was no wind. A twig snapped sharply. She was certain that there were black bears in this area. She envisioned them roaming in the night, snouts raised, identifying her unwelcome scent in their territory. She tried to remember what she had read about bears when they camped in the mountains two years before. Play dead or try fighting them off? She felt for a fallen branch, something she could use to defend herself if she needed to. Her hand grasped a thick piece of wood. She drew it toward herself and clutched it to her chest. She was afraid to move farther, certain that the slightest noise might draw danger.

She lay curled in that position until her hips were aching. Her legs lost their feeling. She closed her eyes and prayed for morning to come soon. She thought sleep was not possible, and yet she succumbed to the need for it.

When she awoke, the sky was slightly lighter through the fullness of the tree canopy. As her eyes adjusted, she tried to stretch her legs and gasped involuntarily. Her right knee was stabbing with pain as it unlocked from the curled position it had held all night. It was as though the dampness had frozen into her joints. She inched her legs out slowly, then tried to rotate her ankles and wiggle her toes. When it appeared that all were in working order, she held her hand against the rough bark of the oak tree and willed herself to sit up.

Taking a naked foot into her hands, she placed her palms over the top and the sole and felt heat start to radiate into her foot. Rubbing back and forth, slowly at first and then with greater purpose, she felt the nerves on top of her foot begin to twinge with irritation. *That's a good sign,* she told herself. *I'm lucky it wasn't any colder. I could have had frostbite, and all because I was so stupid, drinking booze like it was water. I must have been crazy.*

When her feet felt warmer, she stopped and leaned back into the tree. Crows shouted angrily overhead.

And then she heard something. It wasn't much more than a hum really, but she listened closer and let it play through her mind, the sound continuing from a distance through the trees. It swept in, almost like a wave, and then out again. It was traffic. Her heart pounded as she listened, trying to identify the direction. There were few cars on the road this early in the morning, but each one that passed helped her to focus and to narrow down the options. She concentrated. It was to her left and not very far away at all.

She stood and shoved her broken sandal into the back pocket of her jeans. *A souvenir*, she thought wryly. She stepped forward, placing her bare foot between the twigs with caution.

At first, she felt as if the woods were infinite, each tree leading to the next without a pause, but after what felt like endless searching, she came across a ridge where the tree line opened without warning, and she found herself standing at the top of a rock cut, looking down on the dirt service road that ran parallel to the highway. She must have been only a few hundred yards from the highway when she had slept, she thought, though it had taken her ages to walk here in one shoe.

A car sped by on the busier paved road, the driver glancing up at her for a moment, probably wondering why a girl was standing there alone at dawn.

Edging her way down the sharp outcropping of granite, Rica stepped onto the sandy side road with relief. She took off her other shoe and, grateful for the sand under her feet, began walking above the busy highway that cut past the edge of the park. She followed it south to where it curved left and crossed beneath the busier road. She knew that she was almost at the entrance to the main park. Her steps became faster and she felt herself getting close to tears as she began the walk down the long entrance drive to the park gates. A large motor home turned in and drove by, not stopping despite her attempt to flag a ride. She looked down at herself and saw how she must look to others, a girl with dirt and scratches all over herself, walking in bare feet and carrying a pair of muddied broken sandals.

Rica saw the park gates farther up the road. There was a police car parked next to the entrance and a couple of uniformed men talking to the attendant. Then, on the left side of the gate, her parents' van came driving out of the park, toward her.

"Mom!" she cried, waving as though she wouldn't be seen. "Mom!"

The car pulled up sharply next to her, and her mother leapt out and yelled, "Rica! My God, are you all right?"

Rica ran to hug her mother.

"Everyone is searching for you," her mother said. "I was so worried. We all were worried ..."

Her mother held her away at arm's length and looked her over. Rica could tell that she was taking in every detail, from the mud covered bare feet to the welts that were stinging across her face and neck from the whip of small branches. Rica watched as her mother's eyes overflowed with tears.

"I was so afraid we'd never find you. Or ..."

Rica started to cry too and clung to her mother tightly. "I'm so sorry. I was drinking, we all were, and I didn't know what I was doing. I was with Finney ..." She hesitated and then shook her head as though erasing a memory. "I ran off. He was calling me to come back, I could hear him, but I kept running farther into the woods ..." She started to shake and her mother held her again.

"Finney told us everything. He tried to follow you, but when you kept getting deeper into the woods, he couldn't keep up and he went back to find Petra for help. They all looked for you for a long time, but they didn't have enough light and they thought they might lose someone else. Then Petra decided she should drive back, and she told us what had happened. At least she had enough sense to do that."

Rica could see her mother's jaw tighten at the mention of Petra and knew that she must be angry with her for her part in the night's events.

Rica knew that it was no use trying to defend her own behavior or that of her sisters. Not right now. She stepped back and ran her hand through her hair, pulling a leaf from above her left ear. Her face was sore from insect bites and scratches, and she was surprised to see a deep cut and dried blood on her hand.

Her mother's eyes filled with tears again

as she pulled Rica back toward her.

"Oh, Honey ..." She stroked Rica's head and kissed her matted hair.

"I'm okay, Mom. I'm just so sorry," she said again. "I guess that with the drinking ... my judgment was really off." She wondered if she would ever be able to face her parents without feeling shame, and whether they would ever be able to look at her again without remembering what she had put them through.

As she looked over her mother's shoulder, she saw the police officers start walking toward them. Their faces were grim. Rica realized that they weren't approaching her with the relief of having found her safe. It was apparent that someone was in trouble, and from the looks on their faces, she could tell that she was the one.

Chapter 10

After the reunion with her mother, all Rica wanted to do was to go back to the site, climb into the trailer, and go to sleep. Instead, she was subjected to what felt like hours of questioning back at their campsite. The police had not displayed more than a moment of empathy or concern for how Rica was feeling. The search had involved a lot of people and, as they repeated several times, would not have been necessary if Rica and the others had not been drinking illegally and acting irresponsibly. The possibility of underage drinking charges being laid was pointedly mentioned throughout the inquisition.

Her parents had stood by her with a mix

of tears and resolute anger as she recounted the circumstances of her time with Finney. Finney had already explained to them earlier what had happened, but Rica realized that hearing her own version of the evening must have been even harder for them.

After finishing up with Rica, the police had gone to the neighboring site and had spoken again with Finney, who stood nervously next to Alan and Joanne while Craig sat fidgeting on the picnic table. When the officers left, Rica's father had called Finney over and angrily repeated what he had undoubtedly already said more than once – that "no means no." Although Finney was obviously upset and seemed truly sorry for what he had done, her father had still suggested that there may be reason to consider a sexual assault charge.

Finney apologized to Rica and her parents once more before returning to his campsite. Alan and Joanne were packing up to leave; they told Rica's parents that they were anxious to return Finney to his family. Rica suspected that as much as they had always liked Finney, it was unlikely that they would ever forgive him for trying to force himself on their niece.

After the questioning, her mother drove

her into Northbrook for an emergency medical examination to ensure that she hadn't suffered any serious injury or trauma. At the clinic, Rica had felt humiliated as she sat on the edge of the examining table and answered questions about her time alone with Finney. She agreed to an internal examination to reassure her mother that she was fine. The doctor finished her exam and advised them both that Rica was physically unharmed, except for cuts and bruises. They left the clinic and drove back to the park with Rica dozing fitfully in the passenger seat.

When they arrived back at the park, Rica's father was in the middle of unleashing his anger on Kyle and Stefan. It seemed as if no one was exempt from blame. Despite their efforts to help search for Rica during the night, and their obvious relief at finding her home with little more than some scratches and chills, her father was condemning both boys for their irresponsibility. Rica stood awkwardly at the edge of the site as her father, despite his short height, seemed to loom over the taller boys while pacing before them.

"... need to speak to your parents ... don't know what you were thinking ... thought you seemed like responsible boys ... just a child really ..." Although he was berating them for their part in the disastrous night, it became apparent to Rica that her father was berating himself as much as Stefan and Kyle. She could tell that he was angry he had trusted his daughters.

Stefan and Kyle apologized until there was nothing left to say. They sheepishly said good-bye to everyone and walked back to their campsite, probably wondering how long it would take for word to get back to their parents. Rica learned later that the boys were evicted from the park. When the park rangers learned that they were staying at the camp without adult supervision, the boys were given two hours to pack their things and leave.

"And you, Petra," her father then said sternly, turning toward the picnic bench where she sat silently, observing. "Don't ever let something like this happen again. Stealing liquor from your parents! Driving with an open bottle in the car! Wandering off alone with a boy you hardly know, letting your sisters drink, leaving Rica in a vulnerable position ... I can't believe this!"

Rica waited for Petra to explain that Michelle had actually taken the vodka, but

Petra seemed willing to accept responsibility without pointing fingers at anyone else. Although she tried to explain her actions to him once again, it didn't seem to matter what she said; her father held her responsible for the disaster.

Petra's argument with her father had been half-hearted, and Rica could see that she was carrying the burden of knowing that she had suggested the whole plan in the first place, that she had known Michelle was stealing the vodka, that she had watched as Rica drank too much.

It was some time before everyone agreed that enough had been said and that Rica should be in bed. The sun was at its highest as she climbed into the trailer, stripped to her underwear, and slipped gratefully into her sleeping bag. At some point during the afternoon, she rolled over and felt her mother's body beside her, rising and falling in a steady and comforting rhythm. She curled closer and went back to sleep.

* * *

"Petra? Are you awake?"

Rica had woken in the middle of the

night. Her mother had already moved to the opposite side of the trailer and was sleeping soundly next to her father. They were both no doubt exhausted from the previous twenty-four hours. Rica had quietly left the trailer, stepping carefully through the darkness to crawl into the pup tent with her sisters.

It was cool in the nylon tent. She squirmed between the two girls and got under the comforter that lay loosely across the top of their sleeping bags.

"What are you doing?" Petra asked in a sleepy whisper, rolling over to face Rica in the dark.

"I couldn't sleep anymore. I just wanted to talk to you guys and see if you were okay." She felt Michelle stir beside her.

"Yeah, now that we know you're okay, we're okay," Petra said quietly.

"Speak for yourself." Michelle rolled toward them and corrected Petra in a hushed but angry tone. "We're all in shit because of you, Rica. The police found all the empty bottles up at the clearing, and then they smelled it on our clothes, on our breath ..."

"But they aren't placing charges against us," Petra reminded Michelle.

Michelle sat up on one elbow and Rica could almost feel her glaring. "They could have! The only reason they didn't is because Dad said he would guarantee that it would never happen again. Guarantee! You know what that means? It means we're grounded till the end of the century!"

"Don't be so dramatic, Michelle." Petra sounded serious.

"Dramatic? I'm not dramatic; I'm pissed. She's ruined our lives! Dad isn't even letting me run the half-marathon now!"

"I was just trying to fit in," Rica said with a trembling voice. "I'm sorry, you guys," she cried, tears filling her eyes again in what had been possibly the most tear-filled day of her life. "I didn't mean to get anyone in trouble." She started to sob quietly.

"Jeez, Michelle, she didn't get lost on purpose." Petra put an arm across Rica and pulled her over into a sympathetic hug, causing her to cry even harder.

"I don't know how you can forgive her," Michelle said disbelievingly. "You're in even bigger trouble than I am. Dad is blaming us both for letting her drink, but he's never going to forgive you for leaving the baby of the family alone – drunk – so that you could run off with Stefan."

"I know. He's punishing me by taking away my driving privileges," Petra sighed. "He must have told me that a dozen times already. I'll just have to make do. I'll be going away to school next year, anyway. I'll probably live on campus."

"That's nice for you, but I've barely even started driving." Michelle's voice was bitter. "If this affects me – "

"Oh, for God's sake, Michelle. This isn't *about* you; it's about Rica." Petra sat up on her elbow and spoke earnestly through the shadows. "She could have been really hurt. She could still be lost out there. Finney could have done something unthinkable to her – "

"I don't think Finney meant to force me into doing anything," Rica said, wiping her eyes with the blanket. "I don't think he really knew what he was doing, and I kind of encouraged him at first ..."

"Rica," Petra said, her voice serious. "Don't make excuses for him. What would have happened if you hadn't run away? He obviously wasn't listening to you when you told him to stop."

Rica didn't answer. She remembered Finney's groping hands, and she tried to imagine what might have happened if she hadn't managed to push him away. She realized now that there was a lot more at stake when she lay down on that blanket than she had known at the time.

"Dad told Finney that he might have him charged," Rica said quietly. All three girls lay silently contemplating the impact that a sexual assault conviction would have on Finney.

"Do you think he will?" Michelle finally asked. "Lay charges against him?"

Rica sighed. "I don't know. I mean, maybe Finney has learned his lesson already."

"I guess we've all learned something," Petra agreed.

"Yeah, well I learned never to go anywhere with Rica again," Michelle huffed, rolling away from her sister to face the tent wall. "It's just not worth the trouble."

Petra heaved a huge sigh and turned away as well. Rica found herself pinned between their two backsides.

"I don't want to go anywhere with you, anyway," Rica assured Michelle. "You let me down last night. You didn't even come with me to follow Petra and Stefan. If you had followed through with the plan, instead of staying there with Kyle, I wouldn't have even been with Finney, right?"

Michelle was quiet for a moment, and then answered with a heavy sigh. "Look, at that point I'd had way too much to drink, and I thought that maybe hitting on Kyle was revenge enough ... I wasn't thinking straight. But I told you not to go. You just didn't listen to me."

Rica decided that Michelle would never accept any responsibility for what had happened. She lay and thought about how foolish she had been to try and fit in with her sisters and the others when it wasn't in her nature to party. She'd rather stay home with her parents next time and play it safe. Although, she realized, it *had* been a change from the usual vacation. And it *had* been fun, if only for a little while, to try and get back at Stefan.

"Hey, Petra?" she asked suddenly.

"Yeah?" a tired voice answered from the darkness on her left.

"How *was* the swim with Stefan?"

Petra was still for a moment, as if trying to decide whether to discuss it, then rolled onto her stomach and turned her head toward her sister. "Actually, it was nice. Stefan and I talked a lot on the way to the lake, and I know that he was a creep, but he *was* funny and interesting, and it felt exciting going for a swim in the dark. Up until all the trouble started, anyway. A little fun sure wasn't worth all that."

"You know, we looked and looked, but we couldn't find his underwear," Rica giggled. "Did he wear it into the lake?"

Petra laughed shortly. "No, of course not! I told you I could get him to undress. They must have been caught in his jeans when you ran off. We came out of the water, and he just about freaked when he found his clothes were missing. I told him what you guys had done, and we looked around for a while until we heard Finney calling for us and saying he couldn't find you. We had to head up the hill to help him, me pulling on my clothes and poor Stefan walking up behind me with no towel, no clothes – he was frozen and so embarrassed!"

Rica laughed at the vision of Stefan walking up the hill with his hands placed strategically in front of himself.

"It wasn't funny though." Petra's voice turned edgy. "It was cold out and he was wet. What if he had been lost like you were? He could have died of exposure." She shivered. "Anyway," Petra continued, "he stepped on his underwear halfway up the trail. He put them on, and then we found Finney, who gave him the rest of his clothes."

"Oh," Rica said, contrite after Petra reminded her how foolish they had all been.

They lay quietly for some time, and then Michelle's breathing became deep and steady.

"Petra?" Rica said once more. There was no reply. "Thanks for standing up for me. And for getting help for me, even if it meant getting yourself into trouble."

There was no answer, but a moment later Petra's arm reached across Rica's blanketed body and a hand gently squeezed her shoulder.

Chapter 11

The next day, their father made them pack up. He had decided to cut the trip short after everything that had happened. They loaded up the van and left the campsite behind. The long drive home from the park was so unbearably tense that Rica actually wished for Waylon Jennings to be played. This silent ride was almost more than she could stand.

She couldn't wait to be back in her own bedroom, even if she did have to share it with Michelle, and to be back with her own friends, the ones who had interests like her own. *No more attempts to make things exciting or to try to be more like Petra and Michelle,* she thought.

Her mother's voice interrupted her thoughts. "Petra? Did you put the cooler somewhere we can reach? I'd like a cold juice." She was glaring at Petra from the front seat.

"Um, no. Sorry," Petra answered.

Rica turned in her seat to see if she could help by reaching the cooler, but it was buried beneath a mound of boxes and folding chairs. She felt sorry for her sister and wondered if Petra would be blamed for everything from now on.

"I'll stop up here," her father said, indicating a gas station in the distance. "You can buy some juice." He slowed down and put on his turning signal.

"Can we get ice cream?" Michelle asked, looking up from her magazine. Her father looked at her in the rearview mirror, and she slumped down to avoid his glare. *I guess not*, she mouthed to Rica, who tried not to smile.

As they pulled off the highway and stopped next to the pumps, Rica couldn't help but compare this drive to the one just a week ago. There was no hope of switching vehicles this time; Uncle Alan's SUV wasn't following them because he and Aunt Joanne had left the park as soon as the police were finished questioning Finney.

"I'm going into the store," the girls' mother said, and she got out of the van. "Does anyone else need something?"

Rica waited for Michelle to ask again for ice cream, but was surprised when she murmured, "No, thank you."

"I have to use the washroom," Petra said, unfastening her seatbelt and climbing from the vehicle.

"I wonder if everyone at school will find out," Rica said quietly to Michelle, after their father got out of the van to pump the gas.

"Of course they will," Michelle nodded. "Even if we don't say anything, Craig will probably tell everyone. He's really upset with Finney."

"What if they all blame me?" Rica asked worriedly. "They may think it's my fault that Finney got into trouble."

Michelle thought for a moment before looking at Rica. "If anyone blames you, Petra and I will set them straight. Listen, I'm sorry I blamed you for everything. I was just upset about the marathon."

Rica nodded. "Okay."

"And I was pissed about Stefan,"

Michelle went on. "I actually liked him."

"Me too," Rica smiled.

"We must have been crazy. He really wasn't worth the trouble, and look where it got us!"

Rica nodded. "He was a loser," she agreed.

"So now that you've suddenly discovered that there are guys out there," Michelle warned teasingly, "just stay away from my boyfriends, okay?"

Rica realized that although the doctor hadn't detected any physical harm when she was examined, there were definitely some emotional scars left as a result of her experience. She just wasn't ready for any kind of relationship with a boy. She laughed at the idea of competing for Michelle's boyfriends and leaned back in her seat. "Trust me. I'm going to stick to my boring life. I don't need any more excitement and I certainly don't need any boys for a while."

As soon as the words left her mouth, Rica heard the sound of crunching gravel, and turned to look out the van window. A car had pulled up on the other side of the gas pumps. The driver's door opened and a good-looking guy stepped out. Michelle leaned slightly to her right so that she could get a better look at him, and he turned and caught her eye, smiling.

"Oh my God," Michelle said in a hushed voice. "Is he cute, or what?"

Rica nodded silently, and Michelle turned to look at her. Rica watched her sister's expression change to one of concern. For once Michelle actually seemed to be sensitive to her feelings.

"I'm sorry," Michelle said. "Here I am drooling all over the window because of this guy, and you pretty much just told me that you have given up boys forever."

"Forever?" Rica protested. "I didn't say forever. I said for a while. What do I look like, a nun?"

"Well, you do act holier than thou sometimes," Michelle teased as Rica tossed a camp pillow at her.

The two girls were giggling as Petra walked back to the van, glancing appreciatively at the boy before she opened the side door and climbed into her seat.

"What's so funny?" Petra asked, and then followed her sisters' eyes across the pumps. "Oh. Not bad, huh?" she commented.

Rica observed as the two girls leaned back and watched gas being pumped as if it was the most interesting sight they had ever seen. She sighed, crossed her arms, and looked out the window on the other side.

"Did you notice that ugly shirt he's wearing?" Michelle said suddenly, turning to engage Rica in conversation. "That is so last year. And look at his jeans. Way too short. What are they, flood pants?"

"His hair is weird too," Petra commented, picking up on Michelle's cue. "He must cut it himself. He is definitely not a keeper. Who needs him?"

By the time their parents got back in the van, the sisters had stopped paying attention to the unsuspecting boy and were talking together like old friends for once. Rica saw her father give her a look of surprise in the rearview mirror. She wondered if he was thinking that he had lost her to Michelle and Petra and their ways after everything that happened – that she was becoming too close to her older sisters to be considered the baby of the family anymore. *That's never going to happen*, she thought to herself.

"Hey Dad, maybe you could put on some

music," she suggested. "Even a little Waylon Jennings would be okay."

The groans from the other girls were the best reassurance she could offer him.

Here's a sneak peek at
Chelsea's Ride

Friday night television is the worst, Chelsea decided. She was sitting alone, scanning aimlessly through the listings on the screen. She finally settled for watching *Grease* for about the hundredth time. Tossing the remote onto the table in front of her, she picked up her bowl of chips and curled her feet up beside her on the couch.

Her parents had gone away with friends for the weekend, and Leanne and Denny had gone to dinner and a movie. Tara and Sissy had invited her to go to some school dance, but she had said she wasn't interested. Instead, it had seemed to be a perfect opportunity to have Devon over to her empty house. By the time he had called and told her he was sick and needed to go to bed, it was too late to change her plans to anything but a night of television.

Her phone rang and she flipped it open to look at the display screen. She recognized the number as Tara's.

"Hey Tara," she answered happily, grateful for someone to talk to.

Tara's voice was urgent. "Sissy and I are at the dance over at Rydell. You have to get over here!"

Even though music was blaring in the background, Chelsea could hear that her friend's voice sounded strained.

"What's the matter?" Chelsea asked anxiously. "Are you okay?"

"I'm okay," Tara replied pointedly, "but *you* may not be. Devon is here."

"What?" Chelsea bolted up on the couch, nearly spilling the chips from their bowl.

"He's been talking to his ex for, like, ever. And now they're *slow* dancing!"

Chelsea's mind tried to process a dozen thoughts at once. She held the phone in front of her and stared at it as if it might tell her what to do.

"Chels? Chels?" She could hear Tara's voice from a distance.

ISBN-13: 978-1-897073-44-5

Now available from the* NJPP *series.